COPY 2

SIMENON, GEORGES
MAIGRET BIDES HIS TIME

($12.95)

D1229837

Maigret
Bides His Time

GEORGES SIMENON

Maigret
Bides His Time

Translated by Alastair Hamilton

A HELEN AND KURT WOLFF BOOK

HARCOURT BRACE JOVANOVICH, PUBLISHERS

SAN DIEGO   NEW YORK   LONDON

Library of Congress Cataloging in Publication Data
Simeon, George, 1903–
Maigret bides his time.

Translation of: Patience de Maigret.
"A Helen and Kurt Wolff book."
I. Title.
PQ2637.I53P3213   1985   843'.912   83-25134
ISBN 0-15-155563-X

Printed in the United States of America
First American edition 1985
A B C D E

CHAPTER

1

The day had started like a memory of childhood, dazzling and delectable. For no reason, because life was wonderful, Maigret's eyes laughed as he had his breakfast, and the eyes of Madame Maigret, who was sitting opposite him, were just as merry.

The windows of the flat were wide open, letting in the smells from outside, the familiar noises from Boulevard Richard-Lenoir, and the air, already warm, was quivering; a fine vapor filtered the sunrays and made them almost tangible.

"You're not tired?"

He replied with surprise, sipping his coffee, which seemed better than on other days:

"Why should I be tired?"

"All that work you did yesterday in the garden . . . You hadn't touched a spade or a rake for months. . . ."

It was Monday. Monday, July 7. On Saturday night they had taken the train to Meung-sur-Loire, to the little house they had been preparing for several years, for the day when Maigret would be obliged to retire.

In two years and a few months. At the age of fifty-five! As if a man of fifty-five, who had never really been ill and was not handicapped by any infirmity, would suddenly be unable to run the Crime Squad!

What Maigret found most difficult to conceive was that he had lived fifty-three years.

"Yesterday," he corrected her, "I slept most of the time."

"In the sun!"

"With my handkerchief over my face . . ."

What a pleasant Sunday! A stew simmering in the kitchen, with its blue stone tiles, the scent of the St.-John's-wort, which spread through the house, Madame Maigret going from one room to another, a scarf on her head because of the dust, Maigret in his shirt sleeves, his collar open, wearing a straw hat, weeding, digging, hoeing, raking, and finally dropping off to sleep after lunch and the local white wine, in a red-and-yellow-striped deck chair, where the sun soon reached him but could not rouse him.

In the train back, they both felt heavy and sluggish, their eyelids stinging, and with them they carried a smell that reminded Maigret of his youth in the country, a mixture of hay, dry earth, and sweat: the smell of summer.

"More coffee?"

"I'd love some."

Even his wife's checked apron delighted him by its freshness, by a sort of simplicity, just as he was delighted by the glint of the sun on one of the panes of the sideboard.

"It's going to be hot."

"Very."

He would open his windows overlooking the Seine and work in his shirt sleeves.

"What would you say to lobster with mayonnaise for lunch?"

It was pleasant, too, to walk along the street, where the awnings of the shops formed dark rectangles, pleasant to wait for the bus next to a girl in a light dress on the corner of Boulevard Voltaire.

Luck was on his side. An old bus with an open platform drew up to the curb, and he could go on smoking his pipe as he watched the scenery and the figures of the pedestrians glide past.

Why did they remind him of a brightly colored procession that had drawn the whole of Paris when he had just got married and was only a shy young clerk in the Saint-Lazare police station? Some foreign sovereign and his plumed court were riding in landaus, and the helmets of the Republican Guard glimmered in the sun.

Paris had the same smell as today, the same light, the same languor.

He had not thought of retirement then. The end of his career, the end of his life seemed very distant, so distant that he did not worry about them. And here he was preparing the home for his old age!

No melancholy. A rather sweet smile, really. The Châtelet. The Seine. An angler—there was always at least one—near the Pont au Change. Then some lawyers in black robes gesticulating in the courtyard of the Palais de Justice.

Finally the Quai des Orfèvres, whose every stone he knew and from where he had almost been banished.

Less than ten days earlier, a martinet of a Chief Commissioner, who did not approve of inspectors of the old school, had asked him to resign—to retire early, as he more elegantly put it—on the pretext of some rash act the Superintendent was supposed to have committed.

Everything, or almost everything, in the file he had leafed through with a negligent finger, was false, and, for three days and three nights, without even being allowed to make use of his colleagues, Maigret had endeavored to prove it.

Not only had he succeeded, but he had extracted a confession from the perpetrator of the deed, a dentist on Rue des Acacias, who had several crimes on his conscience.

That was all over. After greeting the two policemen on duty, he climbed the wide staircase, entered his office, opened the windows, took off his hat and jacket, and stood contemplating the Seine and its boats as he slowly filled a pipe.

Despite unforeseen events, there were almost ritual movements, which he made automatically, like, once his pipe was alight, pushing open the door of the inspectors' office.

There were gaps in front of the typewriters and telephones because the holidays had started.

"Hello, boys . . . Can you come in for a second, Janvier?"

Janvier was leading the investigation of the burglaries in jewelers' shops, or, rather, in jewelers' windows. The last one had been on Thursday, on Boulevard du Montparnasse, and the criminals had employed methods that had proved effective for over two years.

"Anything new?"

"Hardly anything. Young men, again: aged from twenty to twenty-five, according to the witnesses. Two of them did it, as usual. One broke the window with a tire iron. The other, who had a black bag in his hand, swept up the jewels, with the help of his friend. It was carefully timed. A cream-colored car stopped just long enough to pick up the two men and disappeared in traffic."

"Handkerchiefs over their faces?"

Janvier nodded.

"The driver?"

"The witnesses don't all agree, but it seems he's young, too, very dark hair, and sunburned. There's only one new clue, and that's pretty vague: just before the burglary, a vegetable seller noticed a man, not tall, tough, with a face like a boxer's, standing a few yards away from the jeweler's, as though he were waiting for someone, often looking up at the clock over the window and then checking his wrist watch. According to the woman, he didn't once take his hand out of his right pocket. During the burglary he didn't budge, and, after the cream-colored car had moved off, he got into a taxi."

"Did you show your vegetable seller the photographs of the suspects?"

"She spent three hours with me in Criminal Records. In the end she didn't give a formal recognition of anybody."

"What does the jeweler say?"

"He's tearing the little hair he's got left. Three days earlier, he claims, the burglary wouldn't have mattered much, because he doesn't usually like having valuable jewels on display. Last week he was able to buy a batch of emeralds and on Saturday morning he decided to put them in the window."

Maigret did not yet realize that what was building up in his office that morning was the beginning of the end of a case that was thenceforth to be known at the Quai des Orfèvres as "Maigret's longest investigation."

And so certain facts gradually become legendary. "Maigret's longest interrogation" was still being discussed, for example, and newcomers were told about that interrogation, which had lasted twenty-seven hours, during which the waiter from the Brasserie Dauphine had never stopped bringing up beer and sandwiches.

Maigret was not the only one to question the suspect. Lucas and Janvier took over, perpetually starting from scratch an interrogation that seemed tedious but nevertheless ended in a full confession.

And the recollections all included "Maigret's most dangerous arrest"—the arrest of the gang of Poles in broad daylight, on Rue du Faubourg Saint-Antoine, without a shot being fired, although the men were armed to the teeth and determined to save their skins.

It might in fact be said that the jewel case started twenty years earlier for the Superintendent, when he took an interest in a certain Manuel Palmari, a vagrant from Corsica who had started humbly as a pimp.

It was the time of relief. The old gang leaders, brothel owners before the war, keepers of secret gambling dens, and organizers of spectacular burglaries, had gone into retirement one after the other, on the banks of the Marne, in the South, and, the less lucky ones or the less clever ones, to the prison of Fontevrault.

Young men, thinking they were going to smash everything to smithereens, took over, bolder than their predecessors, and, for a long time, the police force was baffled and kept at bay.

It was the beginning of attacks on cashiers and jewel burglaries in broad daylight, in the middle of the crowd.

A few culprits were eventually arrested. The crimes ceased for a while, resumed and decreased again, to continue with renewed vigor two years later.

"The kids we arrest are only carrying out orders," Maigret had stated ever since the raids began.

Not only were new faces reported each time, but most of those who were arrested had no police record. They were not from Paris either, and appeared to have come up from the provinces, mainly from Marseilles, Toulon, and Nice, for a specific operation.

Only on a couple of occasions had they chosen the big jewelers, on Place Vendôme and Rue de la Paix, who had alarm systems that discouraged criminals.

Their technique had soon changed. They now aimed at unimportant jewelers, no longer in the heart of Paris, but on the outskirts and even in the suburbs.

"Well, Manuel?"

Ten times, a hundred times, Maigret had upbraided Palmari, first at the Clou Doré, the bar he had bought on Rue Fontaine and turned into a luxurious restaurant, and then in the apartment he shared with Aline on Rue des Acacias.

Manuel never let himself be put out, and their meetings could have passed as meetings between two old friends.

"Sit down, Superintendent. What do you want now?"

Manuel was now nearly sixty and, ever since he had been hit by several machine-gun bullets as he was lowering the blind of the Clou Doré, he had never left his little wheelchair.

"Do you know a young man, a real little nuisance, called Mariani, who was born on your island?"

Maigret filled his pipe, because this always lasted a long time. He finally knew every nook of the apartment on Rue des Acacias, above all the little corner room, full of cheap novels and phonograph records, where Manuel spent his days.

"What's this Mariani done? And why pester me again, Superintendent?"

"I've always been straight with you, haven't I?"

"That's true."

"I've even done you little favors. . . ."

That was true, too. Without Maigret's intervention, Manuel would have had a number of difficulties.

"If you want it to continue, tell me . . ."

Manuel occasionally told, or, in other words, gave up an operator.

"You know, it's only a theory. I've never been in trouble and my record's clear. I don't know Mariani personally. I've just heard . . ."

"Who from?"

"I don't know. A rumor . . ."

Since he lost a leg, Palmari hardly saw a soul. He knew his telephone was tapped and he made sure he made only innocent calls.

Moreover, for the last few months, since the revival of the jewel robberies, two inspectors had been permanently posted to Rue des Acacias.

If there were two of them, it was because one had to trail Aline, while his colleague watched the building.

"Oh, well . . . To do you a favor . . . There's an inn near Lagny—I've forgotten its name—that's kept by an old man who's half deaf and his daughter. . . . I believe Mariani is keen on the girl and likes staying there. . . ."

Every time, over the last twenty years, that Manuel had shown signs of increased prosperity, this prosperity had coincided with a revival of the jewel robberies.

"Was the car found?" Maigret asked Janvier.

"In a side street in the Halles."

"Any clues?"

"Nothing. Moers virtually went over it with a microscope."

It was time for the report in the Chief's office, and Maigret joined the other superintendents.

They each summarized the current cases.

"And you, Maigret? These jewelers?"

"Do you know how many jewelers there are in Paris, sir, not to mention the suburban ones? Just over three thousand. Some of them only display jewels and watches of no great value, but on the whole we can say that a good thousand of these shops have something on show to tempt an organized gang."

"What are your conclusions?"

"Let's take the jeweler's on Boulevard du Montparnasse. For months it displayed only mediocre objects. By chance, the other week, the dealer got hold of some valuable emeralds. On Saturday morning he decided to put them on display. On Thursday the window was smashed to bits and the jewels were stolen."

"You think . . ."

"I'm almost certain that a man in the trade makes the rounds of the jewelers, periodically changing districts. Someone is alerted the minute the best pieces are displayed in a good place. Some youngsters who have been taught the technique and who aren't suspected by the police are brought up from Marseilles or elsewhere. Two or three times I set a trap, asking jewelers to show some rare pieces."

"Did the gang fall into it?"

Maigret shook his head and relit his pipe.

"I'm patient" was all he muttered.

The Chief, less patient than he was, did not conceal his displeasure.

"And it's been going on for . . ." he began.

"Twenty years, sir."

A few minutes later Maigret was back in his office, happy to have remained serene and good-humored. Once again he opened the inspectors' door, because he hated calling them on the telephone.

"Janvier!"

"I was waiting for you, Chief. I've just received a phone call . . ."

He came into Maigret's office and shut the door.

"Something unexpected . . . Manuel Palmari . . ."

"Don't say he's disappeared?"

"He's been killed. He was shot in his wheelchair. The Superintendent from the Seventeenth Arrondissement is on the spot and he's informed the Public Prosecutor."

"Aline?"

"Apparently she called the police."

"Come on."

At the door Maigret retraced his steps to take a spare pipe from his desk.

As Janvier drove the little black car up the Champs-Elysées in a halo of light, Maigret retained the slight smile on his lips, the twinkle in his eyes, which he had had since he woke up and which he had seen on the lips and in the eyes of his wife.

And yet, deep within himself, if there was not a feeling of sadness, there was at least a certain nostalgia. The death of Manuel Palmari would not send the world into mourning. Apart, perhaps—and that was not certain—from Aline, who had lived with him for several years and whom he had picked up in the street; apart, too, from certain vagrants who owed him everything, his only funeral eulogy would be a vague:

"He had it coming to him. . . ."

One day Manuel had disclosed to Maigret that he, too, had been a choirboy in his home village, a village so poor, he added, that boys left it at the age of fifteen to get away from the misery. He had wandered around the docks in Toulon, where he was later to be found as a bartender and where he soon realized that women constituted capital that could provide a large income.

Had he one or several crimes on his conscience? Some people made insinuations, but it had never been proved, and one fine day Palmari had become proprietor of the Clou Doré.

He thought he was cunning, and it was true that until the age of sixty he had moved so adroitly that he had never run the risk of being convicted.

Admittedly, he had not escaped the machine-gun bullets, but in his wheelchair, among his books and his records, between the radio and the television, he continued to love life, and Maigret suspected him of loving even more passionately, even more tenderly, this Aline, who called him Daddy.

"You shouldn't see the Superintendent, Daddy. I know the cops and I'm fed up with them. This one's no better than the rest of them. One day, you'll see—he'll use what he pumps out of you against you."

The girl sometimes used to spit on the floor at Maigret's feet, and walk away with dignity, waggling her hard little behind.

Maigret had left Rue des Acacias less than ten days ago and here he was again, in the same building, in the same apartment, where, standing by the open window, he had suddenly had an intuition that had enabled him to reconstruct the crimes of the dentist living across the street.

Two cars were parked in front of the building. A policeman in uniform was standing by the door, and, recognizing Maigret, he saluted.

"The fourth floor, on the left," he murmured.

"I know."

The district Police Superintendent, named Clerdent, stood in the living-room talking to a small, plump man with very fair, tousled hair, white, babylike skin, and ingenuous blue eyes.

"Good morning, Maigret."

Seeing Maigret look at his companion, not knowing whether to shake hands, he added:

"Don't you know each other? . . . Superintendent Maigret . . . Monsieur Ancelin, the Examining Magistrate . . ."

"Pleased to meet you, Superintendent."

"It's my pleasure, Monsieur Ancelin. I've heard a lot about you but I haven't yet worked with you."

"I was appointed to Paris only five months ago. I spent a long time in Lille."

He had a high-pitched voice and, despite his plumpness, seemed far younger than he was. He looked more like one of those students who stay on at the university, in no hurry to leave the Latin Quarter and the easy life. Easy, of course, for those who have a rich daddy.

He was sloppily dressed, his jacket too narrow, his trousers too wide and baggy around the knees, and his shoes needed brushing.

It was said at the Palais de Justice that he had six children, that he had no control over his family, that his old car was about to fall to pieces at any moment, and that to make ends meet he lived in a cheap suburban apartment.

"Immediately after calling the Police Judiciaire, I informed the Public Prosecutor," the Police Superintendent explained.

"Has the Deputy arrived?"

"He'll be here in a minute."

"Where's Aline?"

"The girl who lived with the victim? She's crying, laid out on her bed. The maid's with her."

"What does she say?"

"I didn't find out much, and in the state she's in, I didn't persevere. According to her, she got up at half past seven. The maid only comes in at ten. At eight o'clock Aline brought Palmari his breakfast in bed and then helped him up."

Maigret knew the house routine. Ever since he was disabled, Manuel no longer dared get into a bathtub. He stood under the shower on one leg, and Aline helped him dress.

"What time did she go out?"

"How do you know she went out?"

Maigret would be sure after he had asked his two men on duty in the street. They had not telephoned him. They must have been surprised to see the Police Superintendent arrive, then the Examining Magistrate, and finally Maigret himself, because they did not know what had happened inside the building. There was something quite ironical about it.

"Excuse me, gentlemen."

A tall young man with an equine face burst in, shook hands, and asked:

"Where's the body?"

"In the next room."

"Any clues?"

"I was telling Superintendent Maigret what I know. Aline, the young woman living with Palmari, claims to have left the building around nine, without a hat, and carrying a string bag."

One of the inspectors on duty must have followed her.

"She went to several local shops. I haven't yet had a written statement, because all I could get out of her were disjointed phrases."

"It was when she was out that . . ."

"So she says, of course. She came back at five to ten."

Maigret looked at his watch, which said ten past eleven.

"In the next room she found Palmari, who had slipped from his wheelchair to the carpet. He died after losing a great deal of blood, as you will see."

"What time did she call you? Because I was told she was the one who called the police station."

"Yes. It was a quarter past ten."

The Deputy Public Prosecutor, Alain Druet, asked the questions, while the plump Magistrate listened with a vague smile. He, too, despite the difficulty of feeding his brood, seemed to enjoy life. From time to time he glanced furtively at Maigret, as if to establish a certain complicity.

The two others, the Deputy Public Prosecutor and the Police Superintendent, spoke and behaved like conscientious officials.

"Has the doctor examined the body?"

"He just came in and went out. He claims that it's impossible to tell before the post-mortem how many bullets Palmari received, that it's also impossible to see the bullet holes without undressing him. The bullet through his neck, however, seems to have been fired from behind."

So, thought Maigret, Palmari didn't suspect a thing.

"Let's have a look, gentlemen, before someone from Records gets here."

Manuel's little room had not changed, and the sun flooded in. On the floor was a twisted, almost ridiculous body, and handsome white hair smeared with blood around the neck.

Maigret was surprised to see Aline Bauche standing by the curtain of one of the windows. She was wearing a light-blue linen dress, which he knew, and her black hair framed a pale face covered with red blotches, as though she had been hit.

She looked at the three men with such hatred or such defiance that it seemed as though she were going to pounce on them with her claws out.

"Well, Monsieur Maigret, I suppose you're satisfied?"

Then, to all of them:

"Can't you leave me alone with him, like any woman who's just lost the man in her life? You're probably going to arrest me, aren't you?"

"Do you know her?" the Examining Magistrate asked Maigret in a whisper.

"Pretty well."

"Do you think she did it?"

"You must have been told I never think anything, Monsieur Ancelin. I can hear the men from Records with their equipment. May I question Aline alone?"

"Are you taking her away?"

"I'd rather do it here. I'll tell you what I find out afterward."

"When the body's been removed, it may be necessary to seal

the doors of this room."

"The Superintendent will see to that, if you don't mind."

The Magistrate still looked at Maigret, his eyes full of mischief. Was that how he had imagined the famous Superintendent? Was he disappointed?

"You can have a free hand, but let me know what happens."

"Come along, Aline."

"Where are you taking me? The Quai des Orfèvres?"

"Not so far. To your room. Janvier, go and get our men outside and wait for me in the living room."

With hard eyes, Aline watched the experts invade the room with their equipment.

"What are they going to do to him?"

"The usual. Photographs, fingerprints, and so on. By the way, has the weapon been found?"

She pointed to the table near the sofa, where she used to lie for days on end, keeping her lover company.

"Did you pick it up?"

"I haven't touched it."

"Have you seen this gun before?"

"As far as I know, it belonged to Manuel."

"Where did he keep it?"

"In the daytime he hid it behind the radio, within reach; in the evening he put it on his night table."

A Smith & Wesson .38, the weapon of a professional, which knows no mercy.

"Come along, Aline."

"What for? I don't know anything."

She followed him unwillingly into the living room and

opened the door of a very feminine bedroom, with a huge low bed such as one sees more frequently in the movies than in Parisian houses.

The curtains and hangings were of buttercup silk; a large white goatskin rug covered almost the whole of the floor, while tulle curtains transformed the light from the window into golden dust.

"I'm listening," she said peevishly.

"So am I."

"It can last some time."

She sank into an armchair covered in ivory silk. Maigret did not dare sit on the fragile chairs and did not know whether to light his pipe.

"I know you didn't kill him, Aline."

"No kidding?"

"Don't be unpleasant. You helped me last week."

"That can't be the most intelligent thing I've ever done. The proof is that your two men are always standing across the street, and that the tallest one trailed me again this morning."

"I'm doing my job."

"Doesn't it ever disgust you?"

"Let's stop playing at war. Let's say I'm doing my job just as you're doing yours, and it doesn't much matter if we're on different sides of the fence."

"I've never hurt a soul."

"That's possible. On the other hand, Manuel has just been hurt irreparably."

He saw the tears well up behind the young woman's eyelids, and they seemed genuine. Aline blew her nose clumsily, like a little girl trying to stop sobbing.

"Why must . . ."

"Why must what?"

"Nothing. I don't know. Why must he be dead? Why did they pick on him? As though he wasn't unhappy enough with one leg and living within four walls."

"He had you."

"That made him suffer, too, because he was jealous, and God knows he had no reason to be."

Maigret took a gold cigarette case from the dressing table and offered it open to Aline. She took a cigarette automatically.

"You came back from your shopping at five of ten?"

"The inspector can confirm that."

"Unless you gave him the slip, as you have now and again."

"Not today."

"So you didn't have to contact anyone for Manuel, no instructions to give, no phone calls."

She shrugged her shoulders, automatically brushing away the smoke.

"Did you come up by the main stairs?"

"Why should I have gone up the back stairs? I'm not a servant, am I?"

"You went first to the kitchen?"

"As I always do after shopping."

"Can I see?"

"Open the door. It's opposite, in the hall."

He just glanced in. The maid was making some coffee. Vegetables were piled on the table.

"Did you empty your string bag?"

"I don't think so."

19

"You're not sure?"

"There are some things one does automatically. After what happened, I can hardly remember."

"Knowing you, you then went into the little room to kiss Manuel."

"You know as well as I do what I found."

"What I don't know is what you did."

"First, I think I screamed. I instinctively rushed toward him. Then, I admit, when I saw all that blood I drew back in horror. I couldn't even give him a last kiss. Poor Daddy!"

Tears ran down her face, and she did not think of drying them.

"You picked up the gun?"

"I've already said I didn't. You see! You pretend to believe me, and the moment we're alone together you set traps for me."

"You didn't touch it, even to wipe it?"

"I didn't touch a thing."

"When did the maid arrive?"

"I don't know. She comes up the back stairs and never bothers us when we're in that room."

"You didn't hear her come in?"

"One can't hear from the little room."

"Is she ever late?"

"Frequently. She has a sick son she has to look after before she comes."

"You called the police station only at quarter after ten. Why? And why wasn't the first thing you did to call a doctor?"

"You've seen him, haven't you? Are many people alive in that condition?"

"What did you do in the twenty minutes between finding the body and telephoning? Here's a piece of good advice, Aline: Don't answer too quickly. I know you. You've often lied to me, and I haven't minded. I'm not sure whether the Examining Magistrate feels as I do. And he's going to decide about your liberty!"

She resumed her derisive, common sneer and said:

"That would top everything! Have them arrest me! And people still believe in justice! Do you still believe in it after what happened to you? Do you believe in it?"

Maigret preferred not to answer.

"You see, Aline, these twenty minutes could be of primary importance. Manuel was a careful man. I don't think he kept compromising documents or objects in this apartment, and even less jewels or large sums of money."

"What are you driving at?"

"Didn't you guess as much? One's first reaction on finding a corpse is to call a doctor or the police."

"I suppose I don't have the same reactions as the average mortal."

"You didn't stand immobile in front of the body for twenty minutes."

"For a while, anyway."

"Doing nothing?"

"If you want to know, I started by praying. I know it's idiotic, since I don't believe in their wretched God. And yet there are times when it gets you in spite of yourself. Whether it did any good or not, I said a prayer for the rest of his soul."

"And then?"

"I started walking."

"Where?"

"From the little room to this room and from this room to the door of the little room. I talked to myself. I felt like an animal in a cage, like a lioness robbed of her male and her cubs. Because he was everything for me, both my man and my child."

She spoke passionately as she paced the room as if to reconstruct what she had done that morning.

"It lasted twenty minutes?"

"Perhaps."

"Didn't it occur to you to tell the maid?"

"I didn't even think of her, and I was never at any point aware of her presence in the kitchen."

"You didn't leave the apartment?"

"To go where? Ask your men."

"Very well. Let's assume you've told the truth."

"That's all I do."

She could be kind. She may have had a kind heart, and her love for Manuel may have been sincere. Only, like many others, her past experiences had left her ill-tempered and aggressive.

How could one believe in goodness, in justice, how could one trust men, after the life she had led until she met Palmari?

"We're going to make a little experiment," muttered Maigret, opening the door.

He called:

"Moers! Can you come in with the paraffin?"

It now looked as though the apartment had been taken over by movers, and Janvier, who had brought in Inspectors Baron and Vacher, did not know where to stand.

"Wait a moment, Janvier. Come in, Moers."

The expert had understood and was preparing his instruments.

"Your hand, please."

"What for?"

The Superintendent explained:

"To prove that you haven't used a firearm this morning."

Without blinking she held out her right hand. Then, just in case, the experiment was repeated on the left hand.

"When can you let me know, Moers?"

"In about ten minutes. I've got all I need down in the truck."

"Is it true you don't suspect me and that you do that as routine?"

"I'm almost sure you didn't kill Manuel."

"Then what do you suspect me of?"

"You know better than I do, my dear. I'm in no hurry. It'll come in its own time."

He called Janvier and the two inspectors, who looked ill at ease in this white-and-yellow bedroom.

"It's all yours, boys."

As if she were preparing for battle, Aline lit a cigarette and puffed out the smoke with a disdainful pout.

CHAPTER

2

When he left his house, Maigret certainly did not expect to return to Rue des Acacias, where he had spent so many anxious hours a week earlier. It was nothing but a radiant day, which he began at the same time as several million other Parisians. Still less did he expect to be sitting at a table at about one o'clock in the afternoon with the Magistrate, Ancelin, in a bistro called Chez l'Auvergnat.

Opposite Palmari's, it was an old-fashioned bar with a traditional zinc counter, apéritifs that hardly anybody, except for old men, ever drank, the owner in his blue apron, his shirt sleeves rolled up, his face barred by a fine black mustache.

Sausages, chitterlings, gourd-shaped cheeses, hams with

grayish rinds, as though they had been kept under ashes, hung from the ceiling, and in the window could be seen enormous flat loaves straight from the Massif Central.

Beyond the glass door of the kitchen, the owner's wife worked away in front of her oven, thin and gaunt.

"Is it for lunch? A table for two?"

There was no tablecloth, but over the oilcloth was some crinkled paper, on which the owner added up the bills. One could read, chalked on a slate:

> *Rillettes du Morvan*
> *Fillet of veal with lentils*
> *Cheese*
> *Tarte maison*

The plump Magistrate perked up in this atmosphere, greedily sniffing the thick scent of food. There were only two or three silent customers left, regulars, whom the owner called by name.

For months this had been the headquarters of the inspectors who took turns watching Manuel Palmari and Aline, one of them always ready to follow the young woman the minute she left the building.

For the moment their job seemed over.

"What do you think of it, Maigret? Do you mind if I call you that, although we've only met once? A meeting, as I just said, which I have long wished for. You know, you fascinate me."

Maigret simply muttered:

"Would you like fillet of veal?"

"I like all country food. I'm the son of peasants, too, and my younger brother runs the family farm."

Half an hour earlier, when Maigret left Aline's bedroom, he had been surprised to find the Magistrate waiting for him in Palmari's little room.

By that time Moers had already made his first report to the Superintendent. The paraffin test was negative. In other words, it was not Aline who had fired the shots.

"No fingerprints on the gun, which has been wiped with care. So have the handles on all the doors, including the front door."

Maigret frowned.

"You mean to say the door handle hasn't even got Aline's fingerprints?"

"That's right."

She interrupted:

"I always wear my gloves when I go out, even in the summer, because I hate having damp hands."

"What gloves were you wearing this morning when you did your shopping?"

"White cotton gloves. Look! Here they are."

She took them out of a handbag shaped like a carryall. Some green marks proved that she had handled the vegetables.

"Baron!" called Maigret.

"Yes, Chief."

"Was it you who followed Aline this morning?"

"Yes. She went out shortly before nine, carrying a red string bag as well as the handbag on the table."

"Was she wearing gloves?"

"White gloves, as usual."

"You didn't let her out of your sight?"

"I didn't go into the shops, but she didn't give me the slip for a second."

"No telephone calls?"

"No. At the butcher's she waited for her turn quite a long time, without talking to the women in the queue with her."

"Did you make a note of the time she got back?"

"To the minute. Six minutes to ten."

"Did she seem in a hurry?"

"On the contrary. She seemed to be dawdling and smiling, like someone making the most of a fine day. It was already hot, and I noticed patches of sweat under her arms."

Maigret, too, was sweating, and he felt his damp shirt under his light jacket.

"Call Vacher. Good. Tell me, Vacher, while your colleague was following Aline Bauche, did you stay on duty outside the building? Where were you?"

"By the dentist's house, right opposite, except for the five minutes I took to drink a glass of white wine at Chez l'Auvergnat. You can see the front door of the building very well from the bar."

"Do you know who came in and out?"

"First I saw the concierge, who came to shake out a mat on the doorstep. She recognized me and muttered something, because she hates us and thinks we're insulting her personally by watching the building."

"Then?"

"At about ten past nine a girl came out with a portfolio

27

under her arm. That was Mademoiselle Lavancher, from the family on the first floor on the right. Her father is a Métro inspector. Every morning she goes to an art school on Boulevard des Batignolles."

"And then? Didn't anyone go in?"

"The butcher's boy delivered meat—I don't know to whom. I know him because I always see him at the butcher's shop farther up the street."

"Who else?"

"The Italian woman on the third floor beat her rugs out the window. Then, a few minutes before ten, Aline came back, loaded with shopping, and Baron joined me. We were surprised to see the Police Superintendent arrive a little later, then the Examining Magistrate, and then you. We didn't know what to do. We thought that since we had no orders the best thing to do was to wait on the street."

"By early afternoon I would like to have a complete list, floor by floor, of the tenants of the building, with every member of their families, occupations, habits, and so on. Do it together."

"Should we question them?"

"I'll do that."

Manuel's body had been taken away, and the medical expert was probably performing the post-mortem.

"I must ask you not to leave the apartment, Aline. Inspector Janvier will stay here. Have your men left, Moers?"

"They've finished their job on the spot. We'll have the photographs and an enlargement of the fingerprints around three o'clock."

"Are there some fingerprints in spite of everything?"

"Everywhere, as usual—on the ashtrays, for example, on the radio, the television set, the records, on masses of objects the murderer probably didn't touch and didn't think worth wiping."

Maigret frowned, and noticed that the Magistrate was intently watching his slightest change of expression.

"Shall I send some sandwiches up, boys?"

"No. We'll go and have lunch after you."

On the landing the Magistrate asked:

"Are you having lunch at home?"

"I'm afraid not, despite the lobster waiting for me."

"May I invite you?"

"You don't know the neighborhood as well as I do. I'll invite you, if you don't mind eating Auvergnat food in a bistro."

So they were sitting at a table covered with a paper tablecloth, and the Superintendent occasionally pulled out his handkerchief to mop his brow.

"I suppose you consider the paraffin test conclusive, Maigret? I once studied the scientific methods of investigation, but I must admit I haven't remembered much."

"Unless the murderer wore rubber gloves, his hands certainly carry minute traces of powder, which last for two or three days and which the paraffin test always reveals."

"Don't you think that Aline, whose maid comes for only a few hours a day, wears rubber gloves, if only to do the dishwashing?"

"Probably. We'll soon see."

He started to look at the little Magistrate with curiosity.

"These rillettes are fabulous. They remind me of the ones

we made on the farm when we killed the pig. I believe you usually carry out your investigations alone, Maigret—I mean alone with your colleagues—and wait for more or less definite results before sending your report to the Public Prosecutor and the Examining Magistrate?"

"It's no longer really possible. After the first interrogation, the suspects have the right to have a lawyer present, and the lawyers, who don't much care for the atmosphere at the Quai des Orfèvres, feel more at ease before a magistrate."

"If I stayed behind this morning and wanted to lunch with you, it isn't to check your initiative, believe me, and even less to curb you. As I said, I'm curious about your methods, and from seeing you at work, I'll get an excellent lesson."

Maigret answered the compliment merely with a vague gesture.

"Is it true you have six children?" he asked in his turn.

"I'll have seven in three months."

The Magistrate's eyes were laughing, as though he were cracking a good joke at the expense of society.

"You know, it's very instructive. From their extreme youth, children have the qualities and defects of adults, so that one gets to know men from watching them live."

"Does your wife . . ."

He was going to say:

"Does your wife agree with you?"

But the Magistrate went on:

"My wife's dream is to be a mother rabbit in a hutch. She's never so gay and carefree as when she's pregnant. She grows enormous, and puts on up to sixty pounds, which she bears light-heartedly."

A gay, optimistic Examining Magistrate, eating a fillet of veal and lentils in an Auvergnat bistro as though he had frequented it all his life.

"You knew Manuel well, didn't you?"

"For over twenty years."

"A tough one?"

"Tough and tender; it's hard to say which. When he arrived in Paris after wandering around Marseilles and the Riviera, he was a wild animal. Most of his kind soon get to know the police, the courts, the Assizes, prison.

"But although Palmari lived in that circle, he made sure he was never noticed, and when he bought the Clou Doré, which was only a bistro at the time, he didn't need much coaxing to give us some information about his customers."

"Was he one of your informers?"

"Yes and no. He kept his distance, and said just enough to keep on the right side of us. So he always pretended not to have seen the two men who fired at him when he was about to lower the blind. As if by chance, two killers from Marseilles were bumped off in the South a few months later."

"Did he get on well with Aline?"

"He lived for her. Make no mistake about it, Monsieur Ancelin: despite her origins, that girl is somebody. She's far more intelligent than Palmari was, and if she'd been well managed she could have made a name for herself on the stage or the screen; she could have undertaken anything."

"You think she loved him in spite of the difference in age?"

"I know from experience that for women, for some at any rate, age is of no importance."

"So you do not suspect her of this morning's murder?"

31

"I suspect nobody and I suspect everybody."

There was only one customer left sitting at a table, and two others at the bar, some workmen from the neighborhood. The fillet of veal was delicious, and Maigret did not remember ever having eaten such succulent lentils. He promised himself he would return one day with his wife.

"Knowing Palmari, the gun was in its usual place behind the radio this morning. If it wasn't Aline who killed him, the murderer was somebody whom Manuel trusted implicitly, somebody who probably had a key to the apartment. Well, for all the months that the house has been watched, Palmari hasn't had any visitors.

"It would be necessary to cross the living room, the door to which was always open, to go into the little room and around the wheelchair, in order to get hold of the weapon. If it's a vagrant, he knows about the paraffin test. But I can't see Palmari welcoming a visitor in rubber gloves. And, finally, my inspectors didn't see any suspect go in. The concierge has been questioned and didn't notice anyone. The butcher's boy, who makes his deliveries every day at the same time, is out of the question."

"Could someone have entered the building yesterday evening or last night and hidden in the stairwell?"

"It's one of the things I'm going to check this afternoon."

"You just said you had no idea. Would you resent it if I suspected you, nevertheless, of having an idea at the back of your mind?"

"It's quite true. But it might not lead anywhere. The building has five floors, not counting the ground floor and the attics.

Each floor has two apartments. That constitutes a certain number of tenants.

"For months, Palmari's telephone conversations have always been recorded, and they've always been perfectly innocent.

"I never could believe that that man had entirely withdrawn from circulation. I had Aline followed every time she went out.

"That was how I discovered that she sometimes telephoned from the back of a place where she did her shopping.

"She also periodically managed to give us the slip for a few hours, by the old trick of the double exit—from a big store or on the Métro.

"I have the dates of those telephone calls and the escapes. I compared them with the jewel robberies."

"Do they tally?"

"Yes and no. Not all of them. The telephone calls were frequently five or six days before a jewel robbery. The mysterious escapes, on the other hand, sometimes took place several hours after the robberies. Draw your own conclusions, keeping in mind that these burglaries have nearly all been committed by young men with no record who have come up on purpose from the South or the provinces. Do you want some more tart?"

It was a juicy plum tart, scented with cinnamon.

"If you have some yourself."

They ended their meal with a marc with no label, which must have been at least ninety proof, and which set their cheeks on fire.

"I'm beginning to see . . ." sighed the Magistrate, mopping

his brow in his turn. "What a pity my work keeps me in the Palais de Justice and that I can't follow your investigation step by step. Do you already know how you're going to set about it?"

"I haven't the slightest idea. If I had a plan, I'd have to change it in a few hours. For the time being, I'll deal with the tenants of the building. I'll go from door to door, like a vacuum-cleaner salesman. Then I'll see Aline again. She hasn't said everything and she'll have had time to think, but that doesn't mean she'll be any more talkative than this morning."

They got up after a short argument about the check.

"I invited myself," protested the Magistrate.

"I'm almost at home here," claimed Maigret. "The next time, somewhere else, it'll be your turn."

From behind his bar the owner asked them:

"Have you had a good lunch, gentlemen?"

"Very good."

So good that they both felt a little heavy, particularly once they were in the sun.

"Thanks for the meal, Maigret. Get in touch with me soon."

"I promise."

And as the florid Magistrate slipped behind the wheel of his dilapidated car, the Superintendent went once more into the building, which was becoming more and more familiar to him.

He had had a good lunch. He could still taste the marc. The heat, even if it did make one drowsy, was pleasant, the sun full of gaiety.

Manuel, too, liked good meals, marc, and this drowsiness on fine summer days.

He must now be under a rough sheet in one of the metal drawers of the Forensic Laboratory.

Baron paced the living room whistling. He had taken off his jacket, opened the window, and Maigret guessed that he was in a hurry to have his lunch after a large glass of beer.

"You can go. Put your report on my desk."

The Superintendent saw Janvier, in his shirt sleeves, too, in the little room, where he had lowered the Venetian blinds. When Maigret came in, he got up, put back on its shelf the novel he was busy reading, and grabbed his jacket.

"Has the maid left?"

"I questioned her first. She isn't very talkative. She's new, taken on at the beginning of the week. Apparently the other one went back to the country—to Brittany, I believe, to look after her sick mother."

"What time did she arrive today?"

"At ten o'clock, according to her."

In Paris, as elsewhere, there are several types of maid. This one, Madame Martin, belonged to the most disagreeable category—women who have had misfortunes and continue to attract disasters, so that they hold it against the world in general.

She wore a black, almost shapeless dress, down-at-heel shoes, and she looked at people furtively and fiercely, as though she were always expecting to be attacked.

"I don't know anything," she had told Janvier before he had even opened his mouth. "You have no right to pester me. I've only been working here for four days."

One could tell she was in the habit of muttering vengeful phrases between her teeth during her solitary work.

"I'm leaving, and nobody's going to stop me. I'm never going to put another foot in this house. I suspected they weren't married and that there'd be trouble one day."

"What makes you think that Monsieur Palmari's death has anything to do with his not being married?"

"It's always like that, isn't it?"

"Which stairs did you use?"

"The back ones," she replied bitterly. "Once, when I was young, people would have been pleased to have me come up the main stairs."

"Did you see Mademoiselle Bauche?"

"No."

"Did you go straight into the kitchen?"

"I always start there."

"How many hours a day did you come for?"

"Two hours, from ten to twelve. All morning on Monday and Saturday. But, thank God, I won't be doing a Saturday."

"What did you hear?"

"Nothing."

"Where was the young lady?"

"I don't know."

"Didn't you have to ask for instructions?"

"I'm old enough to know what to do after I've been told once."

"And what did you have to do?"

"Put away the things she had just bought, which were on the table. Then wash the vegetables. Then run the vacuum cleaner around the living room."

"Did you have time to do it?"

"No."

"What came after the living room on other days?"

"The bedroom and the bathroom."

"Not the little room?"

"The gentleman's study? The young lady looked after that herself."

"Did you hear a shot?"

"I didn't hear anything."

"You didn't even hear the young lady's voice on the telephone?"

"The door was closed."

"What time did you see Mademoiselle Bauche this morning?"

"I don't know exactly. Ten minutes or a quarter of an hour after I came in."

"How did she look?"

"She'd been crying."

"She wasn't crying any more?"

"No. She said:

" 'Don't leave me alone. I'm frightened. I'm going to faint. Daddy's been killed.' "

"Then?"

"She went toward her room. I followed her. It was only once she'd fallen onto the bed that she started crying again. Then she said:

" 'Open the door when the bell rings. I've called the police.' "

"You weren't curious enough to ask for details?"

"What people do is none of my business. The less one knows the better."

"You didn't even go and have a look at Monsieur Palmari?"

"Why should I?"

"What did you think of him?"

"Nothing."

"And of the young lady?"

"Nothing either."

"You've been here since Monday. Have you seen any visitors?"

"No."

"Nobody asked to talk to Monsieur Palmari?"

"No. Is that all? Can I go?"

"Provided you leave me your address."

"It's not far. I live in the attic in the shabbiest house on Rue de l'Etoile, 27 *bis*. You'll only find me in in the evening, because I work all day. And remember, I don't like the police."

Janvier had just read the Superintendent this statement, which he had taken down in shorthand.

"Did Moers leave a long time ago?"

"About three-quarters of an hour. He searched everything in this room, examined the books one by one, and the record sleeves. He told me to tell you he didn't find anything. No hiding place in the walls either, and no double drawers in the furniture.

"He ran the vacuum cleaner around just in case and took away the dust to analyze it."

"Go and have lunch. I recommend the fillet of veal at Chez l'Auvergnat, if you can still get some at this hour. Then come back and get me. Did you tell the Superintendent not to say anything to the press?"

"Yes. See you later. Incidentally, was the Magistrate a bore?"

"On the contrary. I'm beginning to like him."

Once he was alone, Maigret took off his jacket, slowly filled a pipe, and started to look around, as if he were taking the place over.

Palmari's wheelchair, which he saw empty for the first time, suddenly seemed impressive, particularly because the leather of the seat and the back bore the imprint of the body, and also the hole from a bullet that had got lodged in the padding.

He automatically fingered the books, the records, turned on the radio for a moment and heard it advertise a brand of baby food.

He pulled up the blinds on the windows, one of which overlooked Rue des Acacias, and the other, Rue de l'Arc-de-Triomphe.

For three years Palmari had lived in this room from morning to night, leaving it only to go to bed, after Aline had undressed him like a child.

According to what he had maintained ten days earlier and what the inspectors had confirmed, he did not have any visitors and, apart from the radio and the television, his companion was his only link with the outside world.

Finally, Maigret crossed the living room and knocked at the door of the bedroom. Receiving no answer, he opened it and found Aline lying on her back on the enormous bed, staring at the ceiling.

"I hope I didn't wake you up?"

"I wasn't asleep."

"Have you had lunch?"

"I'm not hungry."

"Your maid has said she isn't coming back."

"What do I care? If only you wouldn't come back."

"What would you do?"

"Nothing. If you were killed, too, would your wife appreciate having her apartment invaded and being asked question after question?"

"I'm afraid it's essential."

"I can't think of anything more inhuman."

"Yes: murder."

"And you think I committed it? In spite of the test your expert performed this morning?"

"You do your own cooking, I suppose?"

"Like all women who haven't got a cook."

"Do you wear rubber gloves?"

"Not for the cooking, but to clean the vegetables and do the dishwashing."

"Where are they?"

"In the kitchen."

"Can you show them to me?"

She got up unwillingly, her eyes dark with spite.

"Come."

She had to open two drawers before she found them.

"There you are! You can send them to your artists. I didn't wear them this morning."

Maigret put them in his pocket without a word.

"Contrary to what you may think, Aline, I like you very much and even admire you."

"Should I be moved?"

"No. I'd like to have a word with you in Manuel's little room."

"Or else . . . ?"

"What do you mean?"

"If I refuse? I suppose you'll take me to your office in the Quai des Orfèvres?"

"I'd rather it happened here."

She shrugged her shoulders, went ahead of him and sank onto the narrow sofa.

"You think it's going to upset me to see the scene of the crime."

"No. It would be better if you stopped being so stubborn, if you gave up being on the defensive and hiding what you'll have to tell me one day."

She lit a cigarette and looked at Maigret indifferently.

Pointing to the wheelchair, the Superintendent murmured:

"You want whoever did that to be punished, don't you?"

"I'm not counting on the police."

"Would you rather do it yourself? How old are you, Aline?"

"You know. Twenty-five."

"So you have your entire life ahead of you. Did Manuel leave a will?"

"I never asked."

"Did he have a lawyer?"

"He didn't mention one."

"Where did he put his money?"

"What money?"

"What he got from the Clou Doré, to start with. I know

41

it was you who picked up the money due to Manuel from the manager each week. What did you do with it?"

She looked like a chess player imagining all the possible consequences of his next move.

"I put the money in the bank, keeping only what I needed for the household."

"Which bank?"

"The branch of the Crédit Lyonnais on Avenue de la Grande-Armée."

"Is the account in your name?"

"Yes."

"Is there another account in Palmari's name?"

"I don't know."

"Look, Aline. You're an intelligent girl. Up to now, with Manuel, you have been leading a special sort of life, more or less on the fringe of society. Palmari was a gang leader, a tough, who made himself respected for years."

She pointed ironically at the wheelchair, and then at the half-erased patch of blood on the carpet.

"If a man like him, who knew all the ropes, got done in, what do you think will happen to a young woman who is from now on defenseless?"

"Do you want my opinion? I can see only two alternatives. Either whoever had it in for him will soon take care of you, and they won't miss you any more than they missed him. Or else they'll leave you alone, and as far as I'm concerned that will mean that you're in league with them.

"You see, you know too much, and in that set only the dead keep quiet."

"Are you trying to scare me?"

"I'm trying to make you think. We've been trying to get the better of each other for too long."

"Which proves, according to your theory, that I can keep quiet."

"Do you mind if I open the window?"

He opened the one in the shade, but the air outside was hardly cooler than the air in the room, and Maigret went on perspiring. He could not make up his mind whether to sit down.

"For three years you've been living here with Manuel, who, according to him and according to you, had no contact with the outside world. In fact, he had contacts through you.

"Officially you only went once a week, occasionally twice, to check the accounts of the Clou Doré, to pick up Palmari's share and put the money in the bank, in an account in your name.

"But you frequently found it necessary to give my inspectors the slip, either to make some mysterious telephone calls or to have a few hours on your own."

"I might have a lover, for instance?"

"Doesn't it upset you to say something like that today?"

"It's just to show you that there are masses of possibilities."

"No, my dear."

"I'm not your dear."

"I know! You've told me time and again. But even so, there are moments when you behave like a child and one wants to slap you.

"A minute ago I mentioned your intelligence. But you

43

don't seem to be aware of the hornets' nest you've got yourself into.

"That you should have behaved like that as long as Palmari was here to give you advice and protect you is all very well. But from now on you're alone, you hear? Is there another weapon in the house, apart from the one in the hands of the experts?"

"Some kitchen knives."

"You want me to go away, you want me to stop having you watched? . . ."

"That's just what I want."

He shrugged his shoulders, discouraged. Nothing worked with her in spite of her obvious dejection and a certain anxiety, which she did not quite manage to conceal.

"Let's start from another end. Palmari was sixty. For about fifteen years he was proprietor of the Clou Doré, which he ran himself until his infirmity prevented him. From his restaurant alone, he earned a lot of money and he had other sources of income.

"Now, apart from buying this apartment, the furniture, and current expenses, he never spent a great deal. Where is the fortune he amassed?"

"It's too late to ask him."

"Did he have any family you knew of?"

"No."

"Don't you think that loving you as he did he arranged for the money to go to you?"

"You're the one who's said it."

"His kind usually dislike entrusting their money to a bank, because it's too easy to check the date of payments."

"I'm still listening."

"Manuel didn't work alone."

"At the Clou Doré?"

"You know I don't mean that, but the jewels."

"You came to see him about it at least twenty times. Did you get anything out of him? Why do you think that now Daddy's dead you'll succeed with me?"

"Because you're in danger."

"Is that any of your business?"

"I wouldn't like to have to repeat this morning's little ceremony for you."

She seemed to Maigret to be thinking, but nevertheless, as she put out her cigarette in the ashtray, she sighed:

"I've got nothing to say."

"In that case, you'll allow me to leave one of my men in this apartment night and day. Another one will continue to follow you when you go out. Finally, I must ask you officially not to leave Paris before the end of the investigation."

"I see. Where will your inspector sleep?"

"He won't sleep. If you ever have anything to say to me, call me at my office or my home. Here's my number."

She did not touch the card he held out and finally put on the table.

"Now that our talk is over, I can tell you how sorry I am. Palmari had chosen to live on the fringe, but I must admit I rather admired him.

"Good-by, Aline."

The doorbell rang. "It must be Janvier, who's finished his lunch. He'll stay here until I send an inspector to replace him."

He was about to give her his hand. He felt she was upset.

45

But knowing she would not respond to his gesture, he put on his jacket and went to the door to open it for Janvier.

"Anything new, Chief?"

He shook his head.

"Stay here until I send someone to replace you. Watch her, and mind the back stairs."

"Are you going to the Quai?"

After a vague gesture Maigret sighed:

"I don't know."

A few minutes later he was drinking a large beer in a brasserie on Avenue de Wagram. He would have preferred the atmosphere at Chez l'Auvergnat, but there was no telephone booth in the bistro. The telephone hung near the counter, and the customers could hear the conversations.

"Another beer, waiter, and some tokens for the telephone. Make it five."

A bloated prostitute, her face smeared with multicolored make-up, smiled at him ingenuously, without guessing who he was. He felt sorry for her and signaled to her not to waste her time on him.

CHAPTER
3

Gazing vaguely through the windows of the telephone booth at the customers sitting around the tables, Maigret first called the Magistrate, Ancelin, to ask him to postpone fixing seals on the apartment on Rue des Acacias.

"I left one of my inspectors in the apartment and I'm going to send another to spend the night there."

"Have you questioned the young woman again?"

"I've just had a long talk with her, with no result."

"Where are you right now?"

"In a brasserie on Avenue de Wagram, where I still have a few more calls to make."

He thought he heard a sigh. Did the plump little Magistrate

envy him for being deep in the bustle of the city whereas he himself was in a dusty office dealing with abstract files and monotonous formulas?

At school young Maigret used to look nostalgically out the window of his classroom at the men and women coming and going in the street while he was shut in.

The brasserie was almost full, and he was still astonished, after so many years, to see so many people coming and going at times when others were slaving away in offices, shops, or factories.

When he first arrived in Paris, he could spend an entire afternoon outside a café on the Grands Boulevards or Boulevard Saint-Michel, gazing at the moving crowd, watching the faces, trying to guess what everyone was thinking about.

"Thank you, Monsieur Ancelin. The minute there's anything new I'll let you know."

Now for the medical expert, whom he reached in his office. It was no longer Dr. Paul, but his young successor, less picturesque but who nevertheless did his job conscientiously.

"As you know, your men found a bullet in the back of the wheelchair. It was fired from the front, when the victim was already dead."

"From about how far away?"

"Less than a yard and over two feet. I can't be more specific without being theoretical. The bullet that killed Palmari was shot from behind, in the neck, almost point-blank, sloping slightly upward, and was lodged in the brainpan."

"Are the three bullets of the same caliber?"

"As far as I can see. The ballistics expert has them. You'll be getting my official report tomorrow morning."

48

"A last question: the time?"

"Between half past nine and ten."

Now for Gastinne-Renette.

"Did you have time to examine the weapon I sent you and the three bullets?"

"I've got a few more tests to do, but so far it's almost certain that the three bullets were fired from the Smith & Wesson."

"Thank you."

A shy young man in the brasserie walked around in a circle and finally sat next to the prostitute with the thick hips and over-made-up face. Without daring to look at her, he ordered a beer and his fingers tapping the table revealed his embarrassment.

"Hello! Financial Section? Maigret here. Let me talk to Superintendent Belhomme, will you?"

Maigret still seemed more interested in what was going on in the room than in what he was saying.

"Belhomme? Maigret here. I need you, old friend. It's about a certain Manuel Palmari, who lives, or, rather, who lived, on Rue des Acacias. He's dead. Some of his little pals reckoned he'd lived long enough. Palmari owned a restaurant on Rue Fontaine, the Clou Doré, which he turned over to a manager about three years ago. . . .

"Have you got it? He lived with a certain Aline Bauche. She has an account in her name at the branch of the Crédit Lyonnais on Avenue de la Grande-Armée. Apparently she deposited each week part of the returns from the Clou Doré.

"I have reason to believe that Palmari had larger sources of income. Nothing was found in his apartment except for a few notes of a thousand and a hundred francs in his wallet and about two thousand francs in his mistress's handbag.

49

"I don't need to be more specific. The hoard must be somewhere, maybe with a lawyer, maybe invested in some firm or house property. Either I'm wrong, or there's a great deal of it.

"Yes, urgent as always. Thanks, old friend. See you tomorrow."

A telephone call to Madame Maigret, like the one he made that morning.

"I doubt if I'll be back for dinner, and I may only come home very late. . . . Now? . . . On Avenue de Wagram, in a brasserie . . . What are you having to eat? . . . An omelet with fines herbes? . . ."

Finally the Police Judiciaire.

"Let me speak to Lucas, will you? . . . Hello, Lucas? . . . Can you come immediately to Rue des Acacias? . . . Yes . . . And get someone to take over from you at about eight . . . Who's there? . . . Janin . . . Perfect . . . Tell him he'll have to spend a sleepless night . . . No, not outside . . . He'll have a good armchair. . . ."

The young man got up, his cheeks crimson, followed between the rows of tables and chairs by the woman who could have been his mother. Was it the first time?

"A beer, waiter."

Outside, the air was sizzling, and the women looked naked under their light dresses.

If that martinet of a Chief Commissioner could see Maigret now, he would probably have accused him of doing a job unworthy of a superintendent.

And yet that was how the Superintendent had succeeded with most of his investigations: climbing stairs, sniffing in the

50

corners, having a chat here and there, asking apparently futile questions, often spending hours in rather shady bistros.

The little Magistrate had understood and envied him.

A few minutes later Maigret went into the lodge of the building where Aline lived. Concierges are like maids: all good or all bad. He had known charming ones, neat and gay, whose lodges were models of tidiness and cleanliness.

This one, who must have been about fifty-five, belonged to the other category, the ill-tempered, the grumblers, always ready to complain about the wickedness of the world and their sad lot.

"You again?"

She was shelling peas, with a cup of coffee in front of her, on the oilcloth covering the round table.

"What do you want now? I told you I didn't see anyone except the butcher's boy, who's been delivering for several years."

"I suppose you've got a list of the tenants?"

"How else would I get the rent? If only everyone paid on the due day! When I think that I have to climb four or five floors to get to people who don't stint themselves! . . ."

"Will you give me the list?"

"I don't know if I can. Maybe I ought to ask the landlady."

"Has she got a telephone?"

"Even if she didn't, I wouldn't have far to go."

"Does she live in the building?"

"Well! Are you pretending you don't know her? It's too bad if I'm putting my foot in it. This isn't the day to bother her; she's got enough worries as it is."

"You mean? . . ."

"You didn't know? Too bad! You'd have found out sooner or later. When the police start sticking their nose into things . . . Yes, it's Mademoiselle Bauche. . . ."

"Are the receipts signed by her?"

"Who else would have signed them, since the house is hers?"

Without being asked, Maigret had sat down in a wicker armchair, out of which he had driven the cat.

"Let's have a look at the list. . . ."

"So much the worse for you! You'll have to settle it with Mademoiselle Bauche, who isn't always easy."

"Is she tight-fisted?"

"She doesn't care for people who don't pay. And besides, she has her moods."

"I see that the apartment next to yours is occupied by someone named Jean Chabaud. Who is he?"

"A young man in his early twenties who works in television. He's nearly always traveling, because he specializes in sport—football, car racing, the Tour de France. . . ."

"Married?"

"No."

"Does he know Aline Bauche?"

"I wouldn't think so. I had him sign the lease."

"And the apartment on the right?"

"Can't you read? There's a plate on the door: Mademoiselle Jeanine Hérel, chiropodist."

"Has she been living here long?"

"Fifteen years. She's older than I am. She's got a fine practice."

"The first floor on the left, François Vignon . . ."

"Can't one be called Vignon?"

"Who is he?"

"He's in an insurance company, married, two children. The second is only a few months old."

"What time does he leave the building?"

"At about half past eight."

"In the apartment on the right, Justin Levancher."

"Métro inspector. He starts work at six in the morning and wakes me up as he goes by at half past five. An old crosspatch with a liver complaint. His wife's a disagreeable woman, and they'd both do better to watch their daughter, who's only just sixteen."

The second floor on the left: Mabel Tuppler, an American woman, about thirty, living alone and writing articles for American newspapers and magazines.

"No. She doesn't see any men. Men leave her cold. I wouldn't say as much about women."

On the same floor on the right, a retired couple over sixty, the Maupois, who had been in the shoe business, and their maid, Yolande, who lived in the attic. Three or four times a year the Maupoises took a trip to Venice, Barcelona, Florence, Naples, Greece, or somewhere else.

"How do they spend their days?"

"Monsieur Maupois goes out at about eleven to have his apéritif, always dressed up to the nines. In the afternoon, after his siesta, he goes for a walk or shopping with his wife. If only they weren't so mean . . ."

The third floor. On one side a certain Jean Destouches, physical-training instructor at a gymnasium at Porte Maillot.

Goes out at eight in the morning, often leaving in his bed his companion of an evening's or a week's standing.

"I've never seen such a procession. How can one do P.T. if one goes to bed at two nearly every night?"

"Do Destouches and Aline Bauche know each other?"

"I've never seen them together."

"Was he here before she owned the building?"

"He only moved in last year."

"You've never seen Mademoiselle Bauche stop on his floor, go in or out of his apartment?"

"No."

"On the right, Gino Massoletti, representative for France of a make of Italian motorcars. Married to a very pretty woman."

"Butter wouldn't melt in her mouth," added the sour concierge. "As for their maid, who lives in the attic, like the Lavanchers' maid, she's a hot little piece, and I have to open the door for her in the small hours at least three times a week."

The fourth floor: Palmari, or, rather, the late Palmari, on the left, and Aline.

On the same floor, the Barillards.

"What does Fernand Barillard do?"

"Traveling salesman. He represents a deluxe packaging firm, chocolate boxes, almond bags, boxes for perfume bottles. For the New Year he tips me with a bottle of perfume and some marrons glacés, which don't cost him a penny."

"How old is he? Married?"

"Forty or forty-five. Quite a pretty wife, nice and plump, who's always laughing, Belgian, with very fair hair. She sings all day."

"Have they got a maid?"

"No. She does her own housework and shopping, and every afternoon she goes to a tearoom."

"A friend of Aline Bauche?"

"I've never seen them together."

On the fifth floor, Tony Pasquier, second bartender at the Claridge, his wife and two children, eight and eleven. A Spanish maid living in the attic, like the two other maids of the building.

In the apartment on the right, an Englishman, James Stuart, a bachelor. Never goes out before five in the afternoon, and comes back at dawn. No profession. A daily maid in the late afternoon. Frequent visits to Cannes, Monte Carlo, Deauville, Biarritz, and the Swiss resorts in the winter.

"No dealings with Aline Bauche?"

"Why should the whole building have dealings with her? And anyhow, what do you mean by dealings? Do you think they go to bed together? Not one of the tenants even knows she's the landlady."

Just in case, Maigret put a cross against the name of the Englishman, not because he thought he had any connection with the present case, but because he might be an eventual client of the Police Judiciaire. Of the Gambling Squad, for instance.

That left the top floor, in other words, the attics. From right to left, the four maids were: Yolande, the maid of the Maupois, the retired couple on the second floor; the Spanish maid of the Massolettis; the Levanchers' maid; and, finally, the maid of Tony, the bartender.

"Has Stuart been living here long?"

"Two years. He succeeded an Armenian carpet dealer, whose furniture and fittings he bought."

Another tenant of the attic: Mademoiselle Fay, known as Mademoiselle Josette, an old maid who was the oldest tenant of the building. She was eighty-two and still did her own shopping and housework.

"Her room's full of birdcages, which she puts on the window sill in turn. She has at least ten canaries."

An empty room, and then Jeff Claes's room.

"Who is he?"

"A deaf-and-dumb old man who lives by himself. In 1940 he fled from Belgium with his two married daughters and his grandchildren. In the north, in Douai, I think, while they were waiting for a refugee train, the station was bombed, and there were over a hundred killed.

"Hardly anything was left of the daughters and grandchildren. The old man was wounded in the head and face.

"One of his sons-in-law died in Germany; the other remarried in America.

"He goes out only to get something to eat."

The peas had been shelled long ago.

"Now I hope you're going to leave me in peace. I'd just like to know when the body's being brought back and when the funeral's taking place. I have to make a collection for the tenants' wreath."

"We can't settle anything yet."

"Somebody's looking for you. . . ."

It was Lucas, who had entered and stopped by the lodge.

"I can smell the police ten yards away!"

Maigret smiled.

"Thank you!"

"If I answered your questions, it's just because I had to. But I'm no informer, and if everyone minded their own business . . ."

As if to purify the lodge of the fumes Maigret might have left, she went to open the window overlooking the courtyard.

"What shall we do, Chief?" asked Lucas.

"We're going up. Fourth floor on the left. Janvier must be dreaming of a glass of cold beer. Unless Aline's been humanized and has offered him one of the bottles I saw this morning in the refrigerator."

When Maigret rang at the door of the apartment, Janvier, who opened it, had an odd expression. The Superintendent realized why when he entered the living room. Aline went out through the other door, into the bedroom; instead of the light-blue dress she had been wearing in the morning, she wore an orange silk negligee. On a table were two glasses, one half full, some beer bottles, and some playing cards, which had just been dealt.

"You know, Chief, it isn't what you think it is," said the Inspector awkwardly.

Maigret's eyes laughed. He casually counted the hands.

"Belote?"

"Yes. Let me explain. When you left, I insisted on her having something to eat. She wouldn't hear of it and shut herself in her room."

"Did she try to telephone?"

"No. She stayed in bed for about three-quarters of an hour and then came back in a dressing gown, looking nervous, like someone who has tried to sleep and couldn't.

" 'Well, Inspector, it's all very well my being at home, but I'm a prisoner just the same,' she said. 'What would happen if I decided to go out?'

"I thought I was right in replying:

" 'I wouldn't stop you, but an inspector would follow you.'

" 'Are you going to stay all night?'

" 'Not me. One of my colleagues.'

" 'Do you play cards?'

" 'Sometimes.'

" 'Let's play a game of belote to pass the time? It'll help me not to think.' "

"By the way," said Maigret to Lucas, "you ought to call the Quai for one of our men to post himself outside the building. Someone who's not going to be given the slip."

"Bonfils is there. He's the best for this sort of job."

"Tell him to warn his wife he won't be back tonight. Where's Lapointe?"

"In the office."

"Tell him to wait for me here, to come up and stay with you until I come back. Can you play belote, Lucas?"

"Not too badly."

"Aline will probably put you through it, too."

He knocked at the bedroom door, which was opened at once. Aline must have been listening.

"Excuse me."

"You're right at home, aren't you? No point in telling you!"

58

"I'd just like to put myself at your service in case there is anyone you want to inform. The papers won't mention anything before tomorrow, at the earliest. Would you like me to tell the manager of the Clou Doré what happened, for example? Or maybe the lawyer, or some member of the family?"

"Manuel didn't have a family."

"And you?"

"They don't care any more about me than I do about them."

"If they knew you owned a building like this, they'd soon come to Paris, don't you think?"

She registered the blow but did not protest, did not ask any questions.

"Tomorrow there'll be time to call the undertaker, because we can't yet tell when the body will be returned. Do you want it brought back here?"

"He lived here, didn't he?"

"I advise you to eat something. I'm leaving you with Inspector Lucas, whom you know. If you've got anything to say to me, I'll be in the building for a while."

This time the young woman's expression sharpened.

"In the building?"

"I want to meet the tenants."

She watched him as he sent Janvier home.

"I'll have you replaced at about eight or nine this evening, Lucas."

"I asked Janin to come, but I'd rather stay, Chief. If only some sandwiches could be sent up . . . And some beer . . ."

Lucas pointed at the empty bottles.

"Unless there's some left in the refrigerator."

For almost two hours Maigret scoured the building from

top to bottom, from one end to the other, agreeable and patient, with the obstinacy of an expert salesman.

The names he had made a note of in the concierge's lodge progressively ceased to be abstractions, became shapes, faces, eyes, voices, attitudes, human beings.

The chiropodist on the ground floor could just as easily have been a fortuneteller, with her very pale face devoured by almost hypnotic black eyes.

"Why the police? I've never done anything wrong in my life. Ask my clients, who've been coming to me for nine years."

"Somebody died in the building."

"I saw a body being carried out, but I was busy. Who is it?"

"Monsieur Palmari."

"I don't know him. On what floor?"

"The fourth."

"I've heard of him. He's got a very pretty wife, a little affected. I never saw him. Was he young?"

Chabaud, the one who worked in television, was away. The Métro inspector was not back, but his wife was in the apartment with a friend, sitting in front of some cakes and cups of chocolate.

"What can I say? I don't even know who lives above us. If this man never left his apartment, it's not surprising I never met him on the stairs. As for my husband, he never went farther than our floor. Why should he have gone up there?"

Another woman opposite, a baby in its crib, a little girl with a bare behind, on the ground, some baby bottles in a sterilizer.

On the next floor, Miss Tuppler was typing. She was tall, broad, and, because of the heat, was wearing a pair of pajamas with the jacket open. She felt no need to button it up.

"A murder in the building? Gee! How exciting! Have you arrested the murderer? . . . And your name's Maigret? . . . The Maigret of the Quai des Orfèvres? . . ."

She went toward the bottle of bourbon on the table.

"Do you drink?"

He drank, listened to her gibberish for about ten minutes, wondering if she would eventually cover her breasts.

"The Clou Doré? . . . No . . . Never been . . . But in the States nearly all the nightclubs belong to gangsters. . . . Was Palmari a gangster? . . ."

The Superintendent was scouring a sort of condensed Paris, with, from one floor to the next, the same contrasts one finds between districts and streets.

In the American girl's apartment, an untidy bohemian atmosphere reigned. In the apartment of the retired couple opposite, everything was padded, with the softness of jam, and it smelled of candy and jam. A man with white hair was asleep in an armchair, a newspaper on his knees.

"Don't talk too loudly. He hates waking up with a start. Have you come for charitable work?"

"No. I'm from the police."

This seemed to surprise the old lady.

"Really! From the police! In such a quiet house! Don't tell me a tenant's been burgled?"

She smiled, her face gentle and kind, like a nun's under a coif.

61

"A crime? Is that why there's been so much coming and going this morning? No, I don't know anyone except for the concierge."

The physical-training instructor, on the third floor, was out, too, but a young woman, her eyes blurred with sleep, came to open the door, her body wrapped up in a blanket.

"What? No. I don't know when he'll be back. It's the first time I've been here."

"When did you meet him?"

"Last night, or, rather, this morning, since it was after twelve. In a bar on Rue de Presbourg. What's he done? He looked so nice."

No point in persevering. She spoke with difficulty because she had a bad hangover.

At the Massolettis' apartment, there was only the maid, who explained in bad French that her mistress had gone to join her husband at Fouquet's and that they were both having dinner out.

The furniture was modern, lighter and gayer than in the other apartments. A guitar lay on a sofa.

On Palmari's floor, Fernand Barillard was not back. It was a woman of about thirty, with very fair hair, nice and plump, who opened the door, humming.

"Well! I've already passed you on the stairs. What are you selling?"

"Police Judiciaire."

"Are you investigating what happened this morning?"

"How do you know something happened?"

"Your colleagues made enough noise! I just had to open the door a bit to hear what they said. Incidentally, that's a funny way to talk about a dead man, especially the ones who were joking as they carried the body down."

"Did you know Manuel Palmari?"

"I never saw him, but I sometimes heard him roar."

"Roar? What do you mean?"

"He can't have been easy to get along with. I can understand it, because the concierge said he was an invalid. He used to get so angry! . . ."

"With Aline?"

"Is she called Aline? She's pretty odd, anyhow. To begin with, when I met her on the stairs, I used to nod good morning to her, but she looked right through me. What sort of a woman is she? Were they married? Did she kill him?"

"What time does your husband start work?"

"It depends. He hasn't got a set timetable like an office worker."

"Does he come home for lunch?"

"Rarely, because he's usually far away or in the suburbs. He's a traveling salesman."

"I know. What time did he leave this morning?"

"I don't know, because I went out very early to do the shopping."

"What do you call early?"

"About eight. When I came back at half past nine he was no longer here."

"Did you meet your neighbor in the shops?"

"No. We probably don't go to the same ones."

"Have you been married long?"

"Eight years."

Dozens and dozens of questions and as many answers were

63

recorded in Maigret's mind. In the heap, a few, or maybe only one, might suddenly have a meaning.

The bartender was in, because he only started work at six. The maid and the two children were in the first room, which had been turned into a nursery. A child fired at the Superintendent shouting:

"Bang! bang! You're dead!"

Tony Pasquier, whose hair was thick and coarse, was shaving for the second time that day. His wife was sewing a button on a pair of children's trousers.

"What name did you say? Palmari? Should I know him?"

"He's your downstairs neighbor, or, rather, he was your downstairs neighbor until this morning."

"Did something happen to him? I came across some policemen on the stairs, and when I came back at half past two my wife told me a body was carried out."

"Have you ever been to the Clou Doré?"

"Not personally, but I've occasionally sent customers there."

"Why?"

"Some of them ask us where to eat in such and such a district. The Clou Doré has a good reputation. I used to know the headwaiter, Pernelle, who worked in the Claridge. He knows his job."

"You don't know the name of the owner?"

"I never asked."

"And the woman, Aline Bauche, have you ever met her?"

"The girl with black hair and tight dresses I've passed on the stairs?"

"She's your landlady."

64

"That's the first I've heard of it. I've never said a word to her. Have you, Lulu?"

"I hate that type."

"You see, Monsieur Maigret. Not much for you. Maybe you'll be luckier next time."

The Englishman was away. On the seventh floor, the Superintendent found a long hallway lighted by a skylight. On the courtyard side was a huge attic where the tenants stored old suitcases, dressmakers' dummies, chests, a whole lot of junk.

On the side facing the street, the doors were in a row, as in a barracks. He started with the one at the end, belonging to Yolande, the maid of the retired couple on the second floor. It was open, and he saw a transparent nightgown on an unmade bed, some sandals on the rug.

The next door, that of Amelia, according to the plan Maigret had drawn in his notebook, was shut. So was the next one.

When he knocked at the fourth door, a weak voice asked him in and, through the birdcages cluttering the room, he saw, near the window, in a Voltaire chair, a moon-faced old woman.

He almost went out, leaving her to her reverie. She was practically ageless, just connected to the world by a slender thread. She watched the intruder with smiling serenity.

"Come in, my dear sir. Don't be frightened of my birds."

He had not been told that, besides the canaries, an enormous parrot was free, perched on a seesaw in the middle of the room. The bird started shrieking:

"Polly . . . Pretty Polly! . . . Are you hungry, pretty Polly? . . ."

He explained that he was from the police, that a crime had been committed in the building.

"I know. The concierge told me when I went to do my shopping. It's so unfortunate to kill each other when life is so short! It's like war. My father fought in 1870 and in 1914. I, too, have lived through two of them."

"Did you know Monsieur Palmari?"

"Neither him nor anyone else apart from the concierge, who's not as bad as one might think. She's had so many misfortunes, poor woman. Her husband was a philanderer and, to make matters worse, he drank."

"Did you hear any tenant come up to this floor?"

"From time to time people come to fetch or put away something in the attic. But with my window open and my birds singing, you know . . ."

"Do you see your neighbor?"

"Monsieur Jeff? You might think we were the same age. In fact, he's far younger than I am. He can't be much over seventy. It's because of his wounds that he looks older. Do you know him, too? He's deaf and dumb, and I wonder if it isn't worse than being blind.

"Blind people are supposed to be gayer than the deaf. I'll soon know, because my sight gets worse every day and I can't even tell what your face is like. I can only make out a light patch and some shadows. Won't you sit down?"

Finally, the old man, who, when Maigret went in, was reading a children's comic. His face was scarred, and one of the scars drew up the corner of his mouth so he always looked as if he were smiling.

He wore blue glasses. In the middle of the room a large table of white wood was covered with odds and ends, unexpected objects, a little boy's Meccano set, pieces of carved wood, old magazines, clay, out of which the old man had modeled an animal difficult to identify.

The iron bed looked as though it had come from a barracks, as did the coarse blanket. On the whitewashed walls hung colored prints representing sunny towns: Nice, Naples, Istanbul. . . . On the floor were more piles of magazines.

With his hands, which did not shake in spite of his age, the old man tried to explain that he was deaf and dumb, that he could say nothing, and in his turn Maigret gave a sign of helplessness. Then he explained that he could read the words on Maigret's lips.

"I'm sorry to disturb you. I'm from the police. Would you happen to know a tenant named Palmari?"

Maigret pointed to the floor to show that Palmari lived downstairs, held up two fingers to specify the number of floors. Old Jeff shook his head, and the Superintendent spoke about Aline.

As far as he could gather, the old man had met her on the stairs. He described her comically, carving in space her narrow face, her slim, curving figure.

Back on the fourth floor, Maigret felt he had visited a whole universe. He felt heavier, rather sad. Manuel's death in his wheelchair had only caused a very slight stir, and people who had for years been separated from him only by a partition, a floor, or a ceiling did not even know who had been carried away under a sheet.

Lucas was no longer playing cards. Aline was not in the living room.

"I think she's asleep."

Young Lapointe was there, thrilled to be working with the Chief.

"I took a car. Was that all right?"

"Is there any beer left, Lucas?"

"Two bottles."

"Open one for me, and I'll have half a dozen delivered to you."

It was six o'clock. The traffic jams were beginning to form in Paris, and despite the regulations an impatient driver was tooting under the windows of the building.

CHAPTER
4

The Clou Doré in Rue Fontaine was flanked on one side by
a third-rate striptease joint and on the other by a lingerie shop
specializing in highly fanciful female underclothes, which
foreigners took home with them as a souvenir of "Gay Paree."

Maigret and Lapointe, who had left the Police Judiciaire's
car in Rue Chaptal, slowly wandered up the street, where
daytime workers were beginning to mingle with the very
different figures of night life.

It was seven o'clock. The bouncer, whom everyone called
Big-Armed Jo, was not yet at his post, in his blue uniform with
gold braid, on the doorstep of the restaurant.

Maigret, who was looking around for him, knew him well.

He looked like a former side-show boxer, although he had never worn six- or eight-ounce gloves, and, at the age of forty, he had spent half his life in the shade, first as a minor in a reform school, then in prison, serving six months to two years at a time, for petty theft or assault and battery.

He had the intelligence of a child of ten, and in an unexpected situation his eyes became blurred, almost pleading, like those of a schoolboy being asked about a subject he has not studied.

He was indoors, in his uniform, busy passing a rag over the fawn leather seats, and when he recognized the Superintendent, his face had about as much expression as a block of wood.

The two waiters were busy setting the tables, putting on the tablecloths the plates with the crest of the house, glasses, and silver, and, in the middle of each table, two flowers in a crystal vase.

The lamps, with pink shades, were not lighted, because the sun still gilded the sidewalk opposite.

The bartender, Justin, in a white shirt and black tie, gave a last wipe to his glasses. The only customer, a large man with a red face, sitting on a high stool, was drinking a *menthe verte*.

Maigret had seen him somewhere before. It was a familiar face, but he could not place it immediately. Had he met him at the races, or even here, or in his office at the Quai des Orfèvres?

Montmartre was full of people who had had dealings with him, sometimes years earlier, and who vanished for a longer or shorter period of time, either to serve a term at Fontevrault or Melun, or to sink into the background waiting to be forgotten.

"Good evening, sir. Good evening, Inspector," said Justin airily. "If it's for dinner, you're rather early. What can I give you?"

"A beer."

"Dutch, Danish, German?"

The manager came out of the back room silently, his hair scanty, his face pale and rather puffy, mauve rings under his eyes.

With no surprise or apparent emotion he went up to the two men, gave Maigret a soft hand, and then shook Lapointe's hand before leaning against the bar, but not sitting down. He had only to put on his dinner jacket before being ready for his customers.

"I expected you today. I was even surprised you didn't come sooner. What do you think of it?"

He seemed worried and sad.

"What do I think of what?"

"Somebody finally managed to do him in. Have you any idea who it could have been?"

So, although the papers had not mentioned Manuel's death, although Aline had been watched all day and had not made a single telephone call, they knew the news at the Clou Doré.

If a policeman from the Ternes district had talked, it would have been to a reporter. As for the tenants of the building, they did not seem to have any connection with the Montmartre set.

"Since when have you known about it, Jean-Loup?"

The manager, who was also the headwaiter, was called Jean-Loup Pernelle. The police did not know anything against him. Born in the Allier, he had started as a waiter at Vichy. Married young, he was the father of a family; his son studied at the Medical College and one of his daughters had married the owner of a restaurant in the Champs-Elysées. He led a bourgeois life in the house he had had built at Choisey-le-Roi.

"I don't know," he answered in surprise. "Why do you ask? I suppose everyone knows?"

"The papers haven't mentioned the crime. Try to remember. Did you know anything at lunchtime?"

"I think so, yes. The customers tell us so many things! Can you remember, Justin?"

"No. It was mentioned at the bar, too."

"Who by?"

Maigret was up against the law of silence. Even if Pernelle, the manager, did not belong to the set, and led the most orderly of lives, he was no less bound to secrecy by some of his customers.

The Clou Doré was no longer the bar it used to be, where one encountered only vagrants. And Manuel, who had then owned the place, had not needed much coaxing to tip the Superintendent off about them.

The restaurant had acquired some wealthy customers. There was a large number of foreigners, some pretty girls, too, at about ten or eleven at night, because dinner was served until midnight. A few of the gang leaders still stuck to their habits, but they were no longer young and ready for anything. They had houses of their own, and most of them had wives and children.

"I'd like to know the first person to tell you both about it."

And Maigret went fishing, as he put it.

"It wasn't a certain Massoletti?"

He had had time to memorize the names of all the tenants of the building on Rue des Acacias.

"What does he do?"

"He sells cars . . . Italian cars. . . ."

"I don't know him. Do you, Justin?"

"It's the first I've heard of him."

They both seemed sincere.

"Vignon?"

Not a glimmer in their eyes. They shook their heads.

"A physical-training instructor named Destouches?"

"Don't know him here."

"Tony Pasquier?"

"I know him," broke in Justin.

"So do I," continued Pernelle. "He sends me customers sometimes. He's the second bartender at the Claridge, isn't he? I haven't seen him for months."

"He hasn't telephoned today?"

"He only telephones to give a customer a special recommendation."

"Your bouncer wouldn't have heard the news, would he?"

The bouncer, who had overheard, spat on the ground in feigned disgust and muttered between his teeth:

"Well, if that doesn't beat everything!"

"James Stuart, an Englishman? No? Fernand Barillard?"

At each name, the two men looked as though they were thinking and shook their heads once more.

"Who do you think would want to get rid of Palmari?"

"It isn't the first time someone's tried to get him."

"Except that the men who sprayed him with the machine

gun were bumped off. And Palmari never left his apartment. Tell me, Pernelle, when did the Clou Doré change hands?"

A slight blush appeared on the manager's pale face.

"Five days ago."

"Who's the present owner?"

He hesitated only for a second. He realized Maigret knew and that there was no point in lying.

"I am."

"Who did you buy the place from?"

"From Aline, of course."

"How long has Aline been the real owner?"

"I can't remember the date. It's over two years."

"Was the bill of sale made out by a lawyer?"

"It was quite legal."

"Which lawyer?"

"Maître Desgrières, on Boulevard Pereire."

"How much was it?"

"Two hundred thousand."

"New francs, I suppose?"

"Of course."

"Paid in cash?"

"Yes. So it even took some time to count the notes."

"Did Aline take them away in a briefcase or a suitcase?"

"I don't know. I left first."

"Did you know that Manuel's mistress also owns the building on Rue des Acacias?"

The two men were more and more ill at ease.

"There are always rumors. You see, Superintendent, I'm an honest man, like Justin. We've both got a family. Because the restaurant is in Montmartre, we get all kinds of customers. And besides, the law forbids us to throw them out unless they're blind drunk, and that's very rare.

"One hears stories, but one likes to forget them. Isn't that so, Justin?"

"Exactly."

"I wonder," murmured the Superintendent, "whether Aline had a lover."

Neither of them flinched or said either yes or no, which rather surprised Maigret.

"Did she ever meet men here?"

"She didn't even stop at the bar. She came straight up to my office on the mezzanine and checked the accounts like a businesswoman before going off with the amount due to her."

"Aren't you surprised that a man like Palmari apparently transferred to her name all or a good part of what he possessed?"

"Many shopkeepers and businessmen put all their property in their wife's name, for fear of confiscation."

"Palmari wasn't married," objected Maigret. "And there were thirty-five years between them."

"I thought of that, too. You see, I think Manuel was really gone on Aline. He trusted her implicitly. He loved her. I could swear he'd never been in love before he met her. He felt belittled in his wheelchair. She became his life more than ever before, his only contact with the outside world."

"And she?"

"As far as I can see, she loved him, too. It happens to girls like her as well. Before meeting him, she had only met men who had their fun without considering her as a human being, you see? Girls like Aline are far more susceptible than honest women to attention, affection, the prospect of security."

The large, red-faced man at the end of the bar ordered another *menthe*.

"Right away, Monsieur Louis."

And Maigret whispered:

"Who is Monsieur Louis?"

"A customer. I don't know his name, but he comes quite frequently to drink one or two *menthes* with water. I suppose he's from the neighborhood."

"Was he here at midday?"

"Was he here, Justin?" Pernelle repeated in a whisper.

"Just a minute. I think so. He asked me for a tip on some race."

Monsieur Louis mopped his brow and watched his glass gloomily.

Maigret pulled out his notebook and wrote a few words, which he showed Lapointe.

"Follow him if he goes out. Meet you here. If I've left, call me at home."

"Pernelle, while you're not too busy do you mind if we go up to the mezzanine for a minute?"

It was an invitation a restaurant owner can hardly refuse.

"This way . . ."

He had flat feet and waddled along like most elderly head-waiters. The staircase was narrow and dark. There was none of the luxury and comfort of the restaurant. Pernelle pulled a bunch of keys out of his pocket, opened a brown door, and they found themselves in a little room looking onto the court-yard.

The cylindrical desk was covered with bills, pamphlets, two telephones, pens, pencils, and letterhead. On some white wooden shelves was a row of green file boxes and on the wall opposite hung framed photographs of Madame Pernelle, twenty or thirty years younger, a boy of about twenty, and a girl leaning her head forward pensively, her chin in her hand.

"Sit down, Pernelle, and listen to me. Let's play it straight."

"I've always played it straight."

"You know that you haven't, and that you can't or you wouldn't be the owner of the Clou Doré. To put you at your ease I'm going to tell you something that no longer matters for the person concerned.

"When Manuel bought what was only a bistro twenty years ago, I sometimes came here for a drink in the morning, when I was almost sure of finding him alone.

"He also sometimes gave me a call or made a discreet visit to the Quai des Orfèvres."

"An informer?" murmured the manager without much surprise.

"Did you suspect it?"

"I don't know. Maybe. I suppose that's why they shot at him three years ago."

"Possibly. Only, Manuel was clever, and if he occasionally tipped me off about some small fry, he looked after the big jobs himself and hushed them up."

"Don't you want a bottle of champagne sent up?"

"It's about the only drink that doesn't tempt me."

"Some beer?"

"Not for the moment."

Pernelle was obviously suffering.

"Manuel was very clever," Maigret went on, still looking his companion in the eyes. "So clever that I could never get any evidence against him. He knew I knew a great deal of the truth, at least. He didn't bother to deny it. He used to look at me calmly, with a touch of irony, and whenever it was necessary, he handed over one of his confederates."

"I don't understand."

"Yes, you do."

"What do you mean? I never worked for Manuel except here, doing my job as headwaiter and then as manager."

"And yet from twelve o'clock on you knew what had happened to him. As you said, one hears a lot at the bar or in the restaurant. What do you think of the jewel robberies, Pernelle?"

"What I read in the papers: some youngsters trying their hand, who end up by being caught."

"No."

"They mention an older man who's always nearby in case of emergency."

"Then?"

"Nothing. I swear I know nothing else."

"Well, I'll tell you something else, although I'm sure it's not new to you. What is the main risk the jewel burglars run?"

"Being caught."

"How?"

"When they sell."

"Good! You're getting there. All stones of a certain value

have a sort of civil status, and the people in the business know them. The minute a burglary is committed, a description of the jewels is circulated, not only in France but also abroad.

"A receiver, if the burglars know one, will give only ten to fifteen percent of the value of the goods. Nearly always, a couple of years later, when he puts the stones in circulation, the police will identify them and trace them back. Are you with me?"

"I presume that's what happens. You know more about it than I do."

"Well, for years jewels have been disappearing periodically as a result of holdups or window breakings, without ever being found again. What does that mean?"

"How should I know?"

"Come on, Pernelle. One doesn't do your job for thirty or forty years without knowing the tricks of the trade, even if one doesn't take a hand in it."

"I haven't been in Montmartre for so long."

"The first problem is not only to unset the stones, but also to transform them, which entails the complicity of a diamond cutter. Do you know one?"

"No."

"Not many people do, for the simple reason that there aren't many of them around, not just in France but in the world. There aren't more than about fifty in Paris, nearly all living in the Marais, near Rue des Francs-Bourgeois, and they form a very closed little set. Besides, the brokers, the diamond dealers, and the big jewelers who give them work have got their eye on them."

"I hadn't thought of that."

"You don't say!"

There was a knock on the door. It was the bartender, who handed Maigret a slip of paper.

"That's just been dropped off for you."

"Who by?"

"The waiter from the café on the corner."

Lapointe had written in pencil on a page from a notebook:

"He went into the phone booth. Through the window I saw him dial Etoile 42.39. Not sure of the last number. He's sitting in a corner reading a newspaper. I'm staying here."

"Do you mind if I use one of your telephones? By the way, why have you got two lines?"

"I've only got one. The second telephone connects with the restaurant."

"Hello! Directory Assistance? Superintendent Maigret from the Police Judiciaire. I'd like to know, urgently, the name of the subscriber to Etoile 42.39. I'm not sure about the last number. Could you call me back here?"

"Now," he said to Pernelle, "I wouldn't mind a glass of beer.

"Are you sure you don't know any more than what you said about Monsieur Louis?"

Pernelle hesitated, realizing the matter was becoming serious.

"I don't know him personally. I see him at the bar. I've served him sometimes when Justin was away, and we've said a few words about the weather."

"Is he ever with anyone?"

"Hardly ever. I've occasionally seen him with some boys, and I even wondered if he was queer."

80

"You don't know either his surname or his address?"

"I've always heard him called Monsieur Louis, with a certain respect. He must live in the neighborhood, because he never comes by car. . . ."

The telephone rang. Maigret answered.

"Superintendent Maigret? I think I've got the information you wanted," said the girl at Directory Assistance. "Etoile 42.39 has been temporarily discontinued, because the subscriber has gone abroad. The subscriber to Etoile 42.38 is named Fernand Barillard and lives . . ."

The Superintendent knew the rest. The salesman in deluxe packaging who lived on the same floor as Palmari!

"Thank you, miss."

"Don't you want the preceding numbers?"

"Just in case . . ."

He did not know the names or the addresses. Maigret got up heavily, dazed by the heat and an exhausting day.

"Think about what I said, Pernelle. You're your own boss now, and you've got a place that's doing well. It would be too bad to be in trouble, wouldn't it? I feel I'll be seeing you soon. Here's a piece of advice: Don't talk too much, on the telephone or anywhere else, about the conversation we've just had. Incidentally, does deluxe packaging mean anything to you?"

The new owner of the Clou Doré looked at him with genuine surprise.

"I don't understand."

"Certain cardboard manufacturers specialize in chocolate boxes, almond bags, et cetera. Now, this 'et cetera' could include the boxes used by jewelers instead of cases."

He went down the dark and dirty staircase, crossed the

restaurant, where by now a couple sat in a corner and four rather tipsy diners were sitting around a table.

He went up the street to the café and saw Lapointe sitting soberly before an apéritif and Monsieur Louis reading an evening paper in a corner. Neither of them saw him, and a few minutes later the Superintendent got into a taxi.

"Rue des Acacias, corner of Rue de l'Arc-de-Triomphe."

The sky turned a flaming red, coloring the faces of the passers-by. There was not a breath of air, and Maigret felt his shirt sticking to his body. He seemed to be sleeping during the ride and maybe he really was asleep, since he jumped when the driver said:

"We're there, Chief."

He raised his head to look from top to bottom at the light brick building, with the white stone window frames, which must have been built around 1910. The elevator took him to the fourth floor, and out of habit he almost rang at the door on the left.

At the door on the right he was kept waiting for some time, and it was the fair-haired woman he had questioned that afternoon who finally opened it, her mouth full, holding a table napkin.

"You again!" she said, without ill-humor but with surprise. "My husband and I are having dinner."

"I'd like to have a few words with him."

"Come in."

The living room looked like the one opposite, only less luxurious, with a plainer carpet. It did not open onto the sort of little room Palmari had lived in, but onto a bourgeois dining room with homely furniture.

"It's Superintendent Maigret, Fernand."

A man of about forty, his face cut by a dark mustache, got up, also holding his table napkin. He had removed his jacket, undone his tie, and opened his shirt collar.

"Pleased to meet you," he murmured, looking at his wife and then at the visitor.

"The Superintendent came once this afternoon. I didn't have time to tell you. Because of the tenant who died, he went all around the building, ringing at every door."

"Go on eating," said Maigret. "I'm in no hurry."

On the table was some roast veal and noodles with tomato sauce. The couple sat down again to their meal, awkwardly, as the Superintendent sat down at the end of the table.

"Will you have a glass of wine?"

The decanter of white wine, which had just come out of the refrigerator, was misty, and Maigret could not resist. He was right, because it was a wine from Sancerre, both dry and fruity, which had certainly not been bought at a grocer's.

There was an embarrassed silence when the Barillards started eating again under the inscrutable gaze of their guest.

"All I could tell him was that we don't know this Palmari. Personally, I've never set eyes on him, and I didn't even know his name this morning. As for the woman . . ."

Her husband was a handsome man, slim and muscular, who must have been successful with women, and his mustache emphasized greedy lips and impeccable teeth, which showed at the slightest smile.

"Do you know them?"

"No. But let the Superintendent talk. I'm listening, Monsieur Maigret."

He gave the impression of irony, of aggression close to the surface. He was the handsome male, sure of himself, ready for a fight, who doubted neither his charm nor his strength.

"Finish your meal first. Did you have a long round today?"

"In the Lilas district."

"By car?"

"In my car, of course. I've got a Peugeot 404. I'm very pleased with it, and it looks respectable. That's the main thing in my job."

"I suppose you carry a case of samples."

"Naturally, like all my colleagues."

"When you've had your fruit, I'd like you to show it to me."

"Your curiosity is rather unexpected, isn't it?"

"That depends on the point of view."

"May I ask you whether you have made similar requests on the other floors of this building?"

"Not yet, Monsieur Barillard. I must add that you have the right not to agree to my demand, in which case I will call up a very agreeable examining magistrate, who will send a messenger around with a search warrant or, if necessary, a warrant for detention. Maybe you'd rather we continue our talk in my office on the Quai des Orfèvres?"

Maigret did not fail to notice a fairly striking contrast in the two people's attitudes. The woman opened her eyes wide, astonished by the turn the conversation had taken, by the quite unexpected aggression of the two men. Putting her hand on her husband's she asked:

"What's going on, Fernand?"

"Nothing, dear. Don't worry. Superintendent Maigret will soon be apologizing. When the police are faced with a crime they can't understand, they're apt to get nervous."

"Did you receive a telephone call a little less than an hour ago, Madame Barillard?"

She turned to her husband as though she wanted to know what to say, but, without looking at her, he seemed to size up the Superintendent, to guess what he was driving at.

"I had a telephone call."

"From a friend?"

"From a client."

"A chocolate maker? A confectioner? A perfumer? Those are your clients, aren't they?"

"You're pretty well informed."

"Unless it was a jeweler. May I ask you his name, Monsieur Barillard?"

"I must admit I can't remember it, since the matter didn't interest me."

"Really! A client who calls you after work. What did he want?"

"A price list."

"Have you known Monsieur Louis long?"

The blow struck home. Handsome Fernand frowned, and even his wife noticed he was suddenly less at ease.

"I don't know Monsieur Louis. Now if you think we ought to continue our talk, let's go into my study. I'm against

85

bringing women into business on principle."

"Women?"

"My wife, if you'd rather. Do you mind, darling?"

He led him into an adjoining room, about the same size as Manuel's little room, quite comfortably furnished. Since the windows looked onto the courtyard it was darker than the other rooms, and Barillard put on the light.

"Sit down if you want to, and, since I have no alternative, I'm listening."

"You've just said something rather amusing."

"I can assure you my intention is not to amuse you. My wife and I planned to go to the movies tonight, and you're going to make us miss the beginning of the film. What did I say that was funny?"

"That you were against bringing women into business on principle."

"I'm not the only one."

"We'll come to that later. With regard to Madame Barillard, at any rate, I'm prepared to believe you. Have you been married long?"

"For eight years."

"Were you doing the same sort of work as you are now?"

"Just about."

"What was the difference?"

"I worked in a cardboard-box factory in Fontenay-sous-Bois."

"Were you living in this building?"

"I lived in a house in Fontenay."

"Let's see the case of samples."

It was on the floor, to the left of the door, and Barillard hoisted it unwillingly to the desk.

"The key?"

"It isn't locked."

Maigret opened it, and, as he had expected, among the deluxe boxes, nearly all tastefully decorated, he found boxes in which jewelers pack the watches and jewels sold without a case.

"How many jewelers have you visited today?"

"I don't know. Three or four. Watchmakers and jewelers aren't our only clients."

"Do you make a note of the firms you go to?"

For the second time Fernand Barillard winced.

"I haven't got the mentality of an accountant or a statistician. I'm content to write down the orders."

"And of course you keep a copy of these orders made to your firm?"

"Maybe that's what other people do. I trust my employers and like to carry around as little paper as possible."

"So that it's impossible for you to give me a list of your clients?"

"Yes, it's impossible."

"What firm do you work for?"

"Gélot and Sons, on Avenue des Gobelins."

"Their accounts must be in a better state than yours, and I'll pay them a visit tomorrow morning."

"Can you tell me what you're driving at?"

"First, a question. You claim that you never bring women into your business matters, don't you?"

Barillard, who was lighting a cigarette, shrugged his shoulders.

"Even if this woman is called Aline and lives on your doorstep?"

"I didn't know she was called Aline."

"But you knew at once whom I meant."

"There's only one apartment opposite ours, or on our doorstep, and only one woman, as far as I know, in that apartment.

"I've sometimes passed her on the stairs, been in the elevator with her, raised my hat to her, but I don't remember ever having spoken to her.

"Maybe, occasionally, to murmur as I held the elevator door open:

" 'After you . . .' "

"Does your wife know?"

"About what?"

"About everything. About your job. About your various activities. About your relationship with Monsieur Louis?"

"I've told you I don't know a Monsieur Louis."

"And yet an hour ago he told you on the telephone that I was investigating on Rue Fontaine and he reported part of my conversation with the manager of the Clou Doré and the bartender."

"What can I say?"

"Nothing. As you see, I'm doing the talking. There are times when it's better to play it straight, to show your opponent the cards.

"I could have waited to meet your employers and question the accountant on Avenue des Gobelins. Between now and tomorrow they won't be able to fake their books to help you out. And you know perfectly well what I'm going to find."

"Names, addresses, and figures. So many Pompadour boxes at a hundred and fifty francs the dozen. So many . . ."

"So many jewel boxes at so much the dozen or the hundred."

"So what?"

"Imagine, Monsieur Barillard, that I happen to have a list of the jewelers in Paris and the suburbs that have been, for a certain number of years, the objects of major burglaries, whether it be a holdup or, more recently, windows broken with the aid of a tire iron.

"Are you beginning to understand? I am practically sure that, on the list of your clients, which I will receive from the firm Gélot and Sons, I will find almost all the names on my own list."

"And then what? Since I visit most of the jewelers in the district, except the large firms, which use only fancy leather cases, it's normal . . ."

"I doubt if that will be the opinion of the Examining Magistrate in charge of the Palmari case."

"Did my next-door neighbor deal in jewels, too?"

"In his own way. And for the three years he's been an invalid he's been doing it through a woman."

"That's why you just asked me if . . ."

"Exactly. Now I'm asking you if you're Aline Bauche's lover and since when."

It was instinctive. The man could not help glancing at the door, and then crept up to open it a little in order to make sure his wife was not listening.

"If you'd said that in the dining room, I think I'd have

knocked your face in. You have no more right than anyone else to spread suspicion in a family."

"You haven't answered."

"The answer is no."

"And you still don't know a Monsieur Louis?"

"And I don't know a Monsieur Louis."

Maigret reached for the telephone, dialed the number of the apartment opposite, and recognized Lucas's voice.

"What's your client doing?"

"She slept for some time and then she decided to eat a slice of ham and an egg. She gets nervous, paces the rooms, and looks at me murderously every time she goes past."

"She hasn't tried to telephone?"

"No. I'm keeping my eyes open."

"Has anyone been there?"

"No one."

"Thank you. I'll be around in a few minutes. Can you call the Quai in the meantime and tell them to send an extra man? Here, yes. I know Bonfils is downstairs.

"I'd like a second man, and give him the following orders: first, to get a car. Then, to park it by the door and not let the door out of his sight.

"Because I want him to follow a certain Fernand Barillard if he decides to go out alone or with his wife. He's a traveling salesman who lives in the apartment opposite the one you're in.

"I'm there, yes. Have his telephone tapped.

"Barillard's description: about forty years old, five foot seven, thick dark hair, narrow dark mustache, fairly elegant, the sort of man who appeals to women. His wife, if she's with him, is about ten years younger, fair-haired, attractive, rather plump.

"I'll wait here until the inspector arrives downstairs. See you later, old boy."

As he spoke, the salesman looked at him with hatred.

"I suppose," said Maigret almost suavely, "that you still have nothing to say to me?"

"Absolutely nothing."

"My inspector will take about ten minutes to get here. I intend to keep you company in the meantime."

"Just as you like."

Barillard sat in a leather armchair and pretended to be deep in a magazine he had grabbed off a table. Maigret stood up and started to examine the room in detail, reading the titles of the books in the study, lifting up a paperweight, half opening the drawers of the desk.

They were long minutes for the salesman. Over his magazine he occasionally glanced at this thickset, placid man who seemed to fill the whole study with his bulk, crush it under his weight, and on whose face not a thought could be read.

From time to time the Superintendent pulled his watch out of his pocket, because he had never got used to wrist watches and he treasured the gold hunter he had inherited from his father.

"Four more minutes, Monsieur Barillard."

Barillard tried not to flinch, but his hands began to betray his impatience.

"Three minutes."

He controlled himself with more and more difficulty.

"There! I hope you have a good night until our next meeting, which will, I trust, be as cordial as this one."

Maigret left the study and found the young woman in the dining room with red eyes.

"My husband hasn't done anything wrong, has he, Superintendent?"

"You must ask him, my dear. I hope not, for your sake."

"Despite his appearance, he's a very gentle, very affectionate man. He occasionally flares up, but he's always the first to be sorry."

"Good night, Madame Barillard."

She accompanied him to the door with anxious eyes and saw him go, not to the elevator, but to the door opposite.

CHAPTER
5

It was a strained Aline, with a sharp, set expression emphasized by heavy rings under her eyes, who opened the door for Maigret, more placid than ever. In the time it took to cross the hall, he had adopted the good-natured look that his inspectors knew well and that did not deceive them.

"I didn't want to leave the building without wishing you as good a night as possible."

Lucas, sitting in an armchair, put the magazine he was reading on the carpet and got up lazily. It was not difficult to realize that the relationship was by no means cordial between the two people who had just spent several hours shut up in the apartment and were going to stay there until morning.

"Don't you think you ought to go to bed, Aline? You've had quite an emotional day. I'm afraid tomorrow is going to be just as arduous, if not more so. Haven't you got a sleeping pill or some sort of tranquilizer in your medicine cabinet?"

She watched him intently, trying to tell what was at the back of his mind, furious to see that the Superintendent was not giving up.

"For my part, I've found out a great deal since this morning, but I have to check a number of points before discussing my discoveries with you. As a matter of fact, this very evening I met a rather interesting man who lives on your floor.

"At first I was wrong about him: I thought he was just a traveling salesman in boxes for perfume and chocolates.

"It appears that his activity is far broader, and includes the world of jewelers, in particular."

He took his time, filled his pipe pensively.

"What with all that, I haven't had dinner yet. I hope Monsieur Louis will have been patient enough to wait for me at the Clou Doré and that we'll be able to eat together."

Another silence. He pushed the tobacco into his pipe with a familiar movement of the index finger, removed the strand that protruded, and finally struck a match while Aline followed his excessively scrupulous movements with growing impatience.

"A handsome fellow, Fernand Barillard. I'd be surprised if he were satisfied with one woman, especially since his wife seems a little too colorless for him. What do you think?"

"I don't know him."

"Of course, the landlady of a building can't know all her

94

tenants intimately. Particularly since I wonder whether this house is the only one you own.

"I'll know tomorrow from the lawyer, Desgrières, with whom I've made an appointment. This case is so complicated, Aline, that I sometimes think I'm losing my way.

"Anyhow, I've posted a man downstairs in case Barillard wants to go out. And from now on his telephone is tapped, just like yours.

"You see how kind of me it is to warn you? You've probably got nothing to tell me?"

Pursing her lips, she walked with sharp, mechanical steps to the bedroom and slammed the door behind her.

"Is all you've said true, Chief?"

"Just about. Good night. Try to keep awake. Make as much strong coffee as you need, and if anything happens call me at Boulevard Richard-Lenoir. I don't know what time I'll be there, but I'm determined to get some sleep."

Instead of taking the elevator he went slowly down the stairs, imagining the life of the tenants as he passed their doors. Some of them were watching television, and the same voices and music could be heard from several apartments. Stamping feet in Mabel Tuppler's apartment suggested that one or two couples were dancing.

Inspector Lagrume was dozing at the wheel of a Police Judiciaire car, and Maigret vaguely shook his hand.

"Haven't you got a car, Chief?"

"I'll get a taxi on Avenue de la Grande-Armée. Have you got your orders?"

"To follow the man Fernand Barillard."

Maigret did not feel as light as when he had waked up that morning in the apartment quivering with the sun or when, on the rear platform of the bus, he had gorged himself on images of a Paris colored like a children's book.

People had a mania for asking him about his methods. Some of them even thought they could analyze them, and he would look at them with bantering curiosity because they knew more about it than he, who usually improvised at the whim of his instinct.

The Chief Commissioner certainly would not have appreciated what the Superintendent's instinct suggested to him that day, and the little Examining Magistrate, in spite of his admiration, would undoubtedly have frowned.

For example, before questioning Fernand Barillard, Maigret should have assembled as much information as possible about him, compiled a file, gotten the dates he was sure of getting from Gélot and Sons and the details that would eventually be supplied by Maître Desgrières.

He preferred to arouse the anxiety of the salesman, put him voluntarily on his guard, without being watched.

For a moment he had thought he should not say anything to Aline, in order to surprise her the next day by confronting her with her neighbor, and watch her reactions.

He had finally decided to do just the opposite, and from now on she knew that he had established a link between her and the cardboard-box salesman.

They were both watched. They could neither meet nor telephone each other. It was impossible for them to leave the building without being followed.

Were they, in these circumstances, going to have a good

night's sleep? Maigret had done the same thing with Monsieur Louis, letting him know that whatever he said and did was from now on recorded by the police.

It was still impossible to establish a link between these three different characters. All they had in common was anxiety, which Maigret did his best to make as acute as possible for each one.

"To the Clou Doré on Rue Fontaine."

There, too, he had put his cards on the table, or almost. And since he had to eat somewhere, he might as well choose the restaurant that Palmari had owned for such a long time before putting it in Aline's name and then leaving it to Pernelle.

When he went in, he was surprised to find such a lively atmosphere. Nearly all the tables were taken and there was the noise of conversation, interrupted by women's laughs, while the smoke of cigars and cigarettes formed an almost opaque cloud a yard from the ceiling.

In the pink light of the lamps, he saw Monsieur Louis sitting at a table opposite a pretty girl. Lapointe was moping at the bar with a lemon squash.

Pernelle went from customer to customer with a professional smile, shaking hands, leaning over to tell a good story or to take an order, which he then handed to one of the waiters.

Two women perched on barstools were showing off for the benefit of Lapointe, who tried to look elsewhere in embarrassment.

When Maigret arrived, one of them leaned over to her friend, probably to whisper:

"He's a cop!"

So that when the Superintendent reached Lapointe, the latter lost all interest in the eyes of the young ladies.

"Have you had dinner?"

"I had a sandwich in the café, where he stayed over an hour. Then he came back here and waited to eat with that young woman."

"Not too tired?"

"No."

"I'd like you to go on following him. When he goes home, call the Quai and ask someone to relieve you. Do the same thing if he goes to the girl's place, which is possible, or if he takes her to a hotel. You'd better have something to eat with me."

"A beer, Monsieur Maigret?"

"It's a little late, Justin. I've had as much beer as I can carry for today."

He signaled to Pernelle, who got them a little table lit by a golden lamp with a silk shade.

"I recommend the *paëlla* this evening. You could start with *ramequins à la niçoise*. To go with it, a dry Tavel, unless you prefer a Pouilly Fumé."

"We'll take the *paëlla* and the Tavel."

"For two?"

He nodded. During the meal he seemed to be concerned only with the food and the deliciously fruity wine. As for Monsieur Louis, he pretended to have eyes only for his companion, who nevertheless turned around two or three times toward the inspectors and must have been asking him about them.

"The longer I look at him," sighed the Superintendent, "the

surer I am that I know him. That was a long time ago, perhaps ten years or more. He might have had dealings with me when he was young and slim, and his present plumpness may be baffling me."

When it came to the check, Pernelle bent over very professionally and found time to whisper in Maigret's ear:

"I remembered something after you left. Some time ago it was rumored that Palmari owned a hotel on Rue de l'Etoile. It was a call house then, the Hôtel Bussière, or Bessière."

Maigret paid as though he attached no importance to it.

"I'm going there, Lapointe," he whispered a little later. "I don't expect I'll stay long. Good luck!"

Monsieur Louis watched him go to the door. A taxi was cruising by. Ten minutes later Maigret got out opposite the Hôtel Bussière, about a hundred yards from a police station, which did not prevent two or three girls from standing on the street with very obvious intentions.

"Coming?"

He shook his head, found a night porter behind the counter that separated the hall from a little room with a cylindrical desk, a key board, and a camp bed.

"Is it for the night? Are you alone? No luggage? In that case I must ask you to pay in advance. Thirty francs plus twenty percent service charge."

He pushed a book in front of the Superintendent.

"Name, address, number of passport or identity card."

If Maigret had gone up with a girl, he would have avoided these formalities. After the trap that had been set for him two weeks earlier and that had almost made him retire before his time, he preferred not to compromise himself.

99

He wrote his name, his address, the number of his identity card, and left out his occupation. He was handed a key, and the ill-shaven night porter pressed an electric bell, which rang on the next floor.

It was not a maid, but a man in shirt sleeves and a white apron who met him on the first floor, took the key, and looked at the number sulkily.

"Number forty-two? Follow me."

The hotel had no elevator, which accounted for the bad humor of the valet. In second- and third-class establishments, the night staff is frequently composed of grubby specimens of humanity, and it would be quite easy to populate an entire chamber of horrors with them.

Here the valet had a limp, and his face, with its crooked nose, was an ugly yellow, which suggested a ruined liver.

"These stairs! These stairs again!" he muttered to himself. "Whorehouse!"

On the fourth floor he went down a narrow hallway and stopped by room forty-two.

"There you are. I'll get some towels."

Because there were no towels in the rooms, this was the old trick for getting a tip in addition to the twenty percent service charge.

The valet then pretended to make sure nothing was missing, and his eyes finally fell on the fifty-franc note that Maigret was holding ostentatiously between two fingers.

"You mean it's for me?"

He became suspicious, but could not stop his eyes from shining.

"Do you want a pretty girl? You couldn't find what you wanted downstairs?"

"Close the door a minute."

"Hey, you haven't got ideas, I hope? That's odd, you look familiar."

"Maybe I look like somebody? Are you always on night duty?"

"Not me. If I'm on night duty every other week, it's because I go to the hospital for treatment."

"If you sometimes work during the day, I suppose you know the regular clients?"

"I know some of them; others just pass through."

His little red-rimmed eyes went from the banknote to the Superintendent's face, and a furrow crossed his brow, showing an arduous attempt at thought.

"Do you know this woman?" Maigret pulled out of his pocket a photograph of Aline Bauche, which he had had taken without her knowing it seven months earlier.

"I wonder if she ever comes here with a man."

The valet barely glanced at the photograph, and his brow darkened still more.

"Are you kidding me?"

"Why?"

"Because it's a picture of the owner. At least, as far as I know."

"Do you see her frequently?"

"Never at night, anyhow. I sometimes see her in the day-time."

"Has she got a room in the hotel?"

"A room and a sitting room on the first floor."

"But she doesn't use them regularly?"

"I tell you I don't know. We see her. We don't see her. It's none of our business, and we aren't paid to watch her."

"Do you know where she lives?"

"How should I know?"

"And her name?"

"I heard the manager, who's a woman, call her Madame Bauche."

"Does she stay long when she comes to the hotel?"

"It's impossible to tell, because of the spiral staircase that connects the manager's office on the ground floor to the suite on the first."

"Can one get to this suite by the main stairs?"

"Of course."

"Take this. It's yours."

"Are you from the police?"

"Perhaps."

"Hey, you aren't Superintendent Maigret by any chance, are you? I thought I knew you. I hope you aren't going to get the owner into any trouble, because I'll be in trouble, too."

"I promise you you won't be mentioned."

A second note had appeared as if by magic in the hand of the Superintendent.

"For the right answer to one question."

"Let's hear the question."

"When Madame Bauche, as you call her, comes to the hotel, does she meet anyone besides the manager?"

"She doesn't have anything to do with the staff, if that's what you mean."

"That isn't what I mean. In her suite she could see people from outside who don't necessarily go up the spiral staircase but who use the main stairs. . . ."

The note was as tempting as the first one. And Maigret cut the man's hesitations short by the straight question:

"What's he like?"

"I've only seen him occasionally, nearly always in the afternoon. He's younger and slimmer than you."

"Dark hair? A narrow black mustache? Good-looking?"

The valet nodded.

"Did he have a suitcase?"

"Usually, yes. He takes a room on the first floor, always the same one, number seven, the one nearest the suite, and he never stays the night."

The note changed hands. The valet rapidly slipped it into his pocket, but he did not leave immediately, maybe wondering if there were a third question, which would earn him another fifty francs.

"Thank you. I promise you I won't get you into any trouble. I'm leaving in a few minutes."

A bell rang, and the valet rushed out of the room shouting:

"Coming!"

"You weren't too hot?" asked Madame Maigret anxiously. "I hope you had time for lunch and dinner and didn't just have sandwiches?"

"I had an excellent *paëlla* at the Clou Doré. As for lunch, I've forgotten. Oh, yes, I was with a funny little magistrate in an Auvergnat bistro."

He had difficulty getting to sleep, because the characters

who had populated his day returned to haunt him, one by one, and in the foreground was the almost grotesque, curiously twisted bulk of Palmari at the foot of the wheelchair.

For the Examining Magistrate, he was only a victim at the beginning of an investigation that would occupy him for a few weeks. But Maigret had known Manuel at different stages of his career, and although they were on different sides of the fence, subtle, almost indefinable bonds had formed between the two men.

Could it be said that the Superintendent respected the former proprietor of the Clou Doré? The word "respect" was too strong. Judging the man impartially, the experienced inspector could not help holding him in some esteem.

In the same way, he had, from the beginning, been curious about Aline, who had a sort of fascination for him. He tried to understand her, sometimes thought he had succeeded, only to have to defer his judgment immediately.

He finally reached the floating state between sleep and waking, and the figures of his characters got blurred, his thoughts became hazier and more imprecise.

Basically, there was fear. He had often discussed it late at night with Dr. Pardon, who also had experience with men and was not far from sharing his conclusions.

Everybody is afraid. People try to erase children's fear by reading fairy stories, and the minute the child goes to school he is afraid to show his parents a paper with a bad mark.

Fear of water. Fear of fire. Fear of animals. Fear of the dark.

Fear at fifteen or sixteen of choosing the wrong career, of failing in one's life.

In his semiconsciousness, all these fears became like the notes of a muted, tragic symphony, the latent fears we drag behind us to the end: acute fear that makes us scream; fear we laugh about when it's over; fear of accidents, disease, policemen; fear of people, of what they say, of what they think, of the looks they give us when we go by.

A short time ago, as he gazed at the tempting note in the Superintendent's fingers, the sickly valet at the Hôtel Bussière had been divided between the fear of losing his job and temptation. Subsequently, as another note appeared, the same mechanism had been at work.

Was he afraid now, afraid that Maigret would talk, that he would bring him into a matter he suspected was serious and that would lead him into God knows what complications?

Was it from fear, too, that Pernelle, the very recent proprietor of the Clou Doré, had whispered into the Superintendent's ear the address on Rue de l'Etoile? Fear of being pestered by the police, fear of having to close his establishment because of some obscure law.

Wasn't Monsieur Louis frightened, too? Until now he had kept in the background, with no apparent link with Manuel and Aline. Now here he was with the Police Judiciaire on *his* heels, and one can't live to his age in Montmartre without knowing what that means.

Who was more frightened at the moment, Aline or Fernand Barillard?

As late as that morning, no one suspected any connection between the two apartments on the fourth floor. Madame Barillard happily enjoyed her life, without asking any questions, as a housewife looking after the household as well as she could.

Had Aline decided to go to bed? Lucas had virtually dug himself into her apartment, calm and determined. Nothing would make him budge. She could neither go out nor telephone. She suddenly found herself by herself, cut off from the rest of the world.

Would she not rather have been taken to the Quai des Orfèvres, where she could have protested, insisted on having a lawyer of her choice present?

Officially, the police were only with her to protect her.

Two doors, a hall, separated her from the man she had met several times in her secret suite at the Hôtel Bussière.

Did Palmari know? He, too, lived for months with the police opposite his house, his telephone tapped, and, what was more, he was an invalid.

He had nevertheless continued his activities, directing his men through Aline.

It was Maigret's last thought before dropping off completely: Aline . . . Manuel . . . Aline called him Daddy. . . . She who was sarcastic and aggressive with everybody, became tender with the old gang leader and defended him like a tigress.

Aline . . . Manuel . . .

Aline . . . Fernand . . .

Someone was missing. Maigret was no longer lucid enough to remember who was not at the roll call. One of the cogs. He had mentioned it to somebody, maybe to the Magistrate? An important cog, because of the jewels.

Aline . . . Manuel . . . Fernand . . . Count Manuel out, since he was dead . . . Aline . . . Fernand.

Each one revolving in his cage, waiting for an initiative by Maigret.

When he woke up, Madame Maigret opened the window wide and then handed him a cup of coffee.

"Have you slept well?"

"I don't know. I dreamed a great deal, but I can't remember about what."

The same sun as the day before, the same gaiety in the air, in the sky, in the chirping of the birds, in the noises and smells of the street.

It was Maigret who was different, who no longer took part in the joyful song of the day now beginning.

"You seem tired."

"I've got a big day ahead of me and responsibilities to assume."

She had guessed that, the evening before, when he came in, but she had taken care not to ask him any questions.

"Wear your gray pin-striped suit. It's lighter than the other one."

Did he hear? He ate his breakfast automatically, swallowed two cups of black coffee without tasting them. He did not hum in the shower and dressed with a vague expression, forgetting to ask what there was for lunch. His only question was:

"Incidentally, was the lobster good yesterday?"

"There's enough left for a salad."

"Call me a taxi, will you?"

No bus this morning, even one with a rear platform. No landscape, no colored images gliding voluptuously over his retina.

"The Quai des Orfèvres!"

First his office.

"Get me Fernand Barillard . . . Etoile 42.38 . . . Hello, Madame Barillard? . . . Superintendent Maigret here . . . Can I speak to your husband, please. . . . I'll wait, yes. . . ."

His hand automatically leafed through the reports piled on his desk.

"Hello! . . . Barillard? . . . It's me again. . . . Yesterday I forgot to ask you to stay at home this morning and probably most of the day. . . . I know! . . . I know! . . . Too bad! Your clients will wait. . . . No, I have no idea when I'll be seeing you. . . ."

Lucas's account was only a confidential note for the Superintendent and his official report would be made later.

"Nothing important to report. She walked around the apartment until two in the morning, and on several occasions, when she passed near me, I thought she was going to scratch my face. She finally shut herself in her room, and after about half an hour I no longer heard any sound. At eight, when Jarvis relieved me, she seemed to be asleep. I'll call the Quai around eleven to find out if you need me."

Lapointe's report was hardly more interesting. It had been telephoned at three in the morning.

"For Superintendent Maigret. Monsieur Louis and his companion stayed at the Clou Doré until half past eleven. The girl is named Louise Pégasse, nicknamed Lulu the Torpedo, the name under which she appears at the end of the program in a striptease club, the Boule Verte on Rue Pigalle.

"Monsieur Louis accompanied her there. I followed him

and sat at a table next to him. After using the stage door, Lulu reappeared on the stage, and when her act was over she sat at the bar, where she and her colleagues have to encourage the customers to drink.

"Monsieur Louis did not move, did not telephone, never left the room.

"Shortly before three, Lulu whispered a few words in his ear. He got his hat and, one behind the other, we waited in the street. Lulu soon came out. The couple went on foot to a residential hotel on Place Saint-Georges: the Hôtel du Square.

"I questioned the night porter. Louise Pégasse has been living in the hotel for several months. She often comes back with a man, rarely the same one. It's the second or third time Monsieur Louis has followed her to her room. I'm calling from a bistro that is about to close. I'll stay on duty."

"Janvier! Where's Janvier? Hasn't he arrived?"

"He's in the men's room, sir."

Janvier came in.

"Send a man opposite the Hôtel du Square on Place Saint-Georges to relieve Lapointe, who must be dead tired. If he's got nothing new to report, he can go home to bed and call in the late afternoon. I may need him then."

He only just had time to rush to the morning conference, arriving last by a lot. There were conspiratorial glances in his direction, because he had the expression he adopted on big days: his set look, his pipe at an angle, squeezed so tightly between his teeth that he had been known to snap the ebonite tip.

"I'm sorry, sir."

He did not listen to any of the things that were said. When his turn came, he just mumbled:

"I'm continuing the investigation into Palmari's death. If all goes well, I might conceivably break up the jewel-robbery organization at the same time."

"Your same old theory! How many years have you suspected Palmari?"

"Quite a number, I admit."

Other reports were waiting for him, in particular those of Gastinne-Renette and the medical expert. The three bullets that had hit Manuel, one of which had lodged in the back of the wheelchair, had indeed been fired from Palmari's Smith & Wesson.

"Janvier! Come in for a minute."

He gave him instructions to organize the duty roster for Rue des Acacias.

A little later he went through the glass door leading from the Police Judiciaire to the Palais de Justice. He went up two floors before finding the office of the Magistrate, Ancelin, right at the top of the building.

It was one of the offices that had not been modernized, reserved for newcomers, and the Magistrate had to pile his papers on the bare floor and keep the lights on all day.

On seeing Maigret, the plump Magistrate rubbed his hands.

"You can take a few minutes off," he told his clerk. "Sit down, my dear Superintendent. I'm eager to know how far you've got."

Maigret summed up his activities of the day before, and the reports received that morning.

"Do you expect all these scattered elements to fit into something conclusive?"

"Every character implicated in this case is afraid. Everyone, at the moment, is isolated from the others, with no means of communication. . . ."

"I see! I see! Very cunning! Not very regular, on the other hand. I couldn't do anything like that, but I'm beginning to understand your tactics. Now what are you going to do?"

"First, a little round of Rue La Fayette, where they have the diamond market every morning, in a brasserie and in the street. I know a certain number of diamond dealers. It's a place I've often had occasion to visit. Then, for reasons you can guess, I'll be going to the Gélot cardboard-box factory."

"So, if I understand correctly, the case is as follows . . ."

And with a mischievous expression, the Magistrate analyzed the mechanism of the case, which proved that he had spent part of the night studying the file.

"I suppose you think Palmari is at the head of the business. For years, in his bar in Montmartre he came across vagrants of all ages, who used to meet there. The older generation had gradually dispersed all over France, but it had nevertheless retained its contacts.

"In other words, with a well-placed telephone call, Palmari could produce the two or three men he needed for such and such a job. Right?"

Maigret agreed, amused by the Magistrate's excitement.

"Although he was isolated from the world as a result of his accident, nothing stopped him from directing his organization through Aline Bauche. In rapid succession he bought the buildings where he lived with her, and I now wonder whether he had a definite aim when he did that."

"Among other things, it enabled him to give certain tenants notice to leave when he needed a vacant apartment."

"Barillard, for example. Very convenient to have an accomplice on your own floor when you're being watched by the police. Do you think Barillard is capable of recutting precious stones and putting them into circulation?"

"Putting them into circulation, yes. Cutting them, no. Because it's one of the most expert jobs in the world. Barillard reported on the jewelry displays worth having a crack at. In view of his profession, this was easy.

"Through Aline, who periodically gave us the slip and went to the Hôtel Bussière . . ."

"Hence the purchase of the hotel, which was also a good investment."

"Some accomplices used to come up from the provinces for a couple of days. Aline, or maybe Barillard, would wait for them in an appointed place, to take possession of the jewels.

"On the whole, the perpetrators of the smash-and-grab raids could leave without any difficulty, without even knowing who they had been working for, which is why the few vagrants we arrested couldn't tell us a thing."

"So someone is missing."

"Exactly. The diamond cutter."

"Good luck, Maigret. Do you mind if I call you that? Call me Ancelin."

And the Superintendent replied with a smile:

"I'll try. In view of my past dealings with examining magistrates, particularly with a certain Coméliau, I doubt if I'll succeed at once. In the meantime, good day, sir. I'll keep in touch."

It was a Gélot son who answered the telephone when he called the cardboard-box factory on Avenue des Gobelins from his office.

"No, no, Monsieur Gélot. There's nothing to worry about. It's simply a matter of checking something that has nothing to do with the reputation of your firm. You say Fernand Barillard is an excellent salesman and I'm prepared to believe you.

"I would just like to know, for our information only, which jewelers have given him orders over the last two years, for example. I suppose your accounting department will have no difficulty in making out this list, which I'll come and collect at the end of the morning. Don't worry. We know how to be discreet."

In the inspectors' room, he gazed slowly at the faces around him and ended up, as usual, by picking on Janvier.

"Doing anything important?"

"No, Chief. I was finishing a report, which can wait. All this paper work!"

"Get your hat and follow me."

Maigret belonged to the generation that included many men who did not want to drive. He personally feared his absent-mindedness, the brown studies he would fall into during an investigation.

"To the corner of Rue La Fayette and Rue Cadet."

In the police force one of the principles when taking an important step is always to be accompanied. If he had not had Lapointe with him the night before, at the Clou Doré, he would not have been able to have Monsieur Louis followed, and it would probably have taken several days before he got interested in Barillard.

"I'll park the car and join you."

Like him, Janvier knew the precious-stone market. Most Parisians, on the other hand, even those who pass Rue La Fayette every morning, do not suspect that those unassuming-looking men dressed like office clerks, who chat in groups in the street and around the tables of the brasserie, have fortunes' worth of precious stones in their pockets.

These stones, in little bags, pass from hand to hand, without the deals being accompanied by any immediate receipt.

In this closed set, where everyone knows everyone else, trust reigns supreme.

"Hello, Bérenstein!"

Maigret shook hands with a tall, thin man who had just left two companions after pocketing a package of diamonds like an ordinary letter.

"Hello, Superintendent. Another jewel robbery?"

"Not since last week."

"You haven't found your man yet? I've discussed it for at least the twentieth time with my colleagues. Like me, they know all the diamond cutters operating in Paris. As I told you, there aren't many of them, and I'm prepared to answer for them. Not one of them would risk recutting stolen or even suspect stones. Those people have a good nose, believe me! Will you have a beer with me?"

"With pleasure. The moment my inspector has crossed the street."

"Well, Janvier! You've arrived promptly, I see."

They sat around a table, and some dealers stood talking between the rows. Occasionally one of them pulled a magnifying glass out of his pocket to examine a stone.

"Before the war the two main stonecutting centers were Antwerp and Amsterdam. Curiously enough, for reasons I haven't yet discovered, most of the stonecutters were, or still are, from the Baltic—Latvia or Estonia.

"In Antwerp they had foreigners' identity cards, and when they retreated before the German advance, they were all directed to Royan and then to the United States.

"After the war, the Americans did what they could to keep them. They hardly managed to keep a tenth of them, because they were all homesick.

"And yet some of them, when they came back, were seduced by Paris. You'll find them in the Marais and Saint-Antoine. Each of them is known, has a sort of pedigree, because it's a trade that is handed down from father to son and that has its secrets."

Maigret suddenly looked at him vaguely, as though he were no longer listening.

"Wait. You said . . ."

A word Bérenstein had said had struck him.

"What did I say that worries you?"

"Just a minute! The German advance . . . The stonecutters from Antwerp . . . The United States . . . Some of them staying there . . . And why couldn't some have stayed in France at the time of the exodus?"

"It's possible. Since they're almost all Jews, they might well have ended up in concentration camps or ovens."

"Unless . . ."

The Superintendent suddenly got up.

"Off we go, Janvier! Where's your car? Good-bye, Béren-stein. I'm sorry. I should have thought of it earlier. . . ."

And Maigret slipped as fast as he could past the groups crowding the sidewalk.

CHAPTER

6

Janvier looked straight ahead, squeezing the steering wheel of the little black car slightly tighter than usual, and he had to resist his desire to watch the face of Maigret, sitting next to him. Once, he opened his mouth to ask a question that was scalding his lips, but he had enough self-control to say nothing.

Although he had been working for the Superintendent ever since he joined the Police Judiciaire and had collaborated with him in hundreds of investigations, he was nevertheless impressed each time the phenomenon, which had just been set in motion, was produced.

The day before, Maigret had plunged into the case with a light-hearted frenzy, producing characters out of the dark, turning them this way and that in his large paws like a cat with a mouse, and then putting them back in their corners. He sent inspectors left and right, as though he had no definite plan, telling himself something would always emerge.

Suddenly he was no longer playing. Janvier was sitting next to another person, a human bulk that nothing could affect, an almost terrifying monolith.

At the end of the morning, the avenues, the streets of Paris, were a real firework in the July heat. There were splashes of light everywhere. They burst from the slate and red-tiled roofs, from the windowpanes, where a red geranium sang: they ran off the multicolored bodies of motorcars, blue, green, yellow, they even seemed to come from the horns, the voices, a squeal of brakes, the ring of a bell, the shrill whistle of a policeman.

It was as though the black car were as resistant to this symphony as an island of silence and immobility, as though Maigret himself were an impassive block, and he certainly saw nothing, heard nothing, did not even notice that they had arrived at Rue des Acacias.

"We're here, Chief."

He stepped heavily out of the car, which had become too narrow for him, gazed blankly at the familiar street, then raised his head, looking as though he were going to take over the whole building, its floors and its occupants.

Yet he took the time to empty his pipe on the sidewalk by tapping it on his heel, and to fill another and light it.

Janvier did not ask if he should go with him, nor did he say anything to Janin, who was watching the building and wondered why the Chief did not seem to recognize him.

Maigret made for the elevator, and Janvier followed him.

Instead of going up to the fourth floor, the Superintendent went on to the fifth, and strode on up to the attics.

Turning to the left, he stopped at the door of the deaf-and-dumb man, and, knowing he would receive no answer, he turned the knob. The door opened. The Fleming's room was empty.

The Superintendent almost ripped off the curtain on the wardrobe and made a short inventory of the few clothes he found in more or less poor condition.

His eyes photographed every corner of the room, after which he went down a floor, hesitated, and plunged once again into the elevator, which took him to the ground floor.

The concierge was in her lodge, a shoe on her right foot, a slipper on her left foot.

"Do you know if Claes has gone out this morning?"

Seeing him so tense impressed her deeply.

"No. He hasn't come down yet."

"You haven't left your lodge?"

"Not even to do the stairs. My neighbor did them for me because I've got my pains again."

"He didn't go out last night?"

"Nobody went out. I only opened the door to tenants coming home. Anyhow, you've got your man in the street and he can tell you."

Maigret was thinking hard, thinking tough, according to the expression Janvier had invented for his own use.

"Tell me . . . Each tenant has a part of the attic at his disposal, as far as I can see. . . ."

"Exactly. And as a rule they can each rent an additional maid's room."

"That's not what I'm asking. And the cellars?"

"Before the war, there were only two large cellars and everyone put his own coal in his own corner. During the war, when hard coal got as expensive as caviar, quarrels broke out, and all the tenants claimed their heaps were getting smaller. Anyhow, the landlord at that time had partitions built, with doors and padlocks."

"So every tenant has his own cellar."

"Yes."

"Claes, too?"

"No. He's not a proper tenant, since he lives in a maid's room."

"And the Barillards?"

"Of course."

"Have you got the keys to the cellars?"

"No. I've just said they've got padlocks. Each tenant has his own."

"Can you see who goes down to the cellars?"

"Not from here. The cellar stairs are opposite the back stairs, down there. You just have to push the door with nothing written on it, with no doormat."

Maigret went back to the elevator and looked Janvier in the eye without saying anything. He did not have the patience to ring at Barillard's door but rapped violently with his fist. Madame Barillard, in a cretonne dress, opened it with a frightened face.

"Your husband?"

"He's in his study. He says you won't let him go to work."

"Call him in."

Barillard's silhouette could be seen, still in pajamas and a dressing gown. Despite his efforts, he did not look as well or as self-confident as the day before.

"Get the key to the cellar."

"But . . ."

"Do as I say."

It was all happening in unreality, in a dream, or, rather, a nightmare. Suddenly the relationship between the protagonists was no longer the same. It seemed as though everyone was in a state of shock and that words had changed value, as had movements and looks.

"Go ahead."

He pushed him into the elevator, and on the ground floor ordered shortly:

"To the basement."

Barillard became increasingly irresolute, Maigret firmer and firmer.

"Is this the door?"

"Yes."

A single, very weak electric bulb lit up the white wall, the doors with faded numbers and obscene graffiti could barely be distinguished on the peeling paint.

"How many keys open this padlock?"

"I've only got one."

"Who might have the other?"

"How should I know?"

"You haven't given the key to anyone?"

"No."

"Are you and your wife the only people who use this cellar?"

"We haven't used it for years."

"Open it."

The hands of the traveling salesman were shaking, and down here he looked more grotesque than in the bourgeois surroundings of his apartment.

"Well? Open it!"

The door had moved about a foot and then stuck.

"There's something behind it."

"Push harder. Use your shoulder."

It was Maigret whom Janvier gazed at in bewilderment, suddenly realizing that the Superintendent expected—but since when?—the present turn of events.

"It's giving way."

Suddenly a leg could be seen hanging. The door, as it opened, released another leg. A body was suspended in midair, the bare feet about a foot and a half above the mud floor.

It was old Claes, wearing a shirt and an old pair of trousers.

"Handcuff him, Janvier."

The Inspector stared at the hanged man and Barillard in turn. When the latter saw the handcuffs, he protested.

"Just a minute, please."

But Maigret's inscrutable eyes weighed on him, and he surrendered.

"Go and get Janin. He's no longer necessary outside."

As he had done upstairs, Maigret inspected the long narrow room, and one felt that every detail was being eternally lodged in his memory. With his finger he touched several tools, which he pulled out of a bag, and then he seemed to caress, thoughtfully, a heavy steel table fastened to the floor.

"Stay here, Janin, until those gentlemen arrive. Don't let

anyone in. Not even your colleagues. And don't touch anything yourself either. Understood?"

"Understood, Chief."

"Let's go."

He looked at Barillard, his silhouette different now that his hands were tied behind his back and he walked like a puppet.

They did not take the elevator, but went up the back stairs to the fourth floor without meeting anybody. Madame Barillard, in her kitchen, screamed when she saw her husband in handcuffs.

"Monsieur Maigret!"

"I'll see you in a minute, Madame Barillard. I've got some telephone calls to make first."

And, taking no notice of the others, he went into Barillard's study, which smelled of stale cigarette smoke, and dialed the Magistrate's number.

"Hello! . . . Yes, it's Maigret. I'm a fool, my dear Monsieur Ancelin. And I feel responsible for the death of a man. Yes, another corpse. Where? On Rue des Acacias, of course. I should have realized from the start. I was beating about the bush instead of sticking to the only important clue. The worst of it all is that this third element, if I can call it that, has been worrying me for years.

"Forgive me if I don't give you any details right now. There's a hanged man in the cellar. The doctor will undoubtedly discover that he didn't hang himself, that he was dead or wounded when the noose was put around his neck. It's an old man.

"May I ask you to make sure that the Public Prosecutor

doesn't come in too much of a hurry? I'm very busy on the fourth floor and I'd just as soon not be disturbed before getting some results. I don't know how long that will take. See you later. Oh, no, we won't be having lunch in that nice Chez l'Auvergnat today."

A little later he had his old friend Moers on the line, the expert from the Criminal Records Office.

"I need a very intricate job done and I don't want it done in a rush. There's no point in the Public Prosecutor and the Examining Magistrate fiddling with everything in the cellar. You'll find some objects that will surprise you. You might have to examine the walls and search the floor."

He got up from Barillard's chair with a sigh, crossed the living room, where Barillard sat in a chair opposite Janvier, who was smoking a cigarette. Maigret went into the kitchen, opened the refrigerator.

"May I?" he asked Madame Barillard.

"Tell me, Superintendent . . ."

"Just a minute, if you don't mind. I'm dying of thirst."

As he opened a beer bottle, she handed him a glass, both submissive and frightened.

"You don't think my husband . . ."

"I don't think anything. Come with me."

She followed him in bewilderment into the study, where he automatically sat in Barillard's chair again.

"Sit down. Make yourself comfortable. Your name is Claes, isn't it?"

"Yes."

She hesitated, blushing.

"Look, Superintendent. I suppose it's important?"

"From now on, Madame Barillard, everything is important. I admit that every word counts."

"I am named Claes. It's my maiden name, written on my identity card."

"But?"

"I don't know if it's my real name."

"Was the old man who lived in the attic a relative?"

"I don't think so. I don't know. It all happened so long ago! And I was only a little girl."

"When do you mean?"

"When Douai was bombed, at the time of the exodus. Trains and more trains, which we got out of to sleep on the ballast. Women carrying wounded babies. Men with arm bands running in every direction, and the train leaving again. Finally, the explosion that seemed like the end of the world."

"How old were you?"

"Four? A little over or a little under?"

"Where does the name Claes come from?"

"I suppose it belonged to my family. Apparently that's what I said."

"And the Christian name?"

"Mina."

"Did you speak French?"

"No. Only Flemish. I'd never seen a town."

"Can you remember the name of your village?"

"No. But why aren't you talking about my husband?"

"I will in time. Where did you meet the old man?"

"I'm not sure. What happened just before and just after the

explosion is very vague. I think I was walking along with someone holding my hand."

Maigret took the receiver off the telephone and asked for the town hall in Douai. He was connected immediately.

"The Mayor is away," said the town clerk.

He was very surprised to hear Maigret ask:

"How old are you?"

"Thirty-two."

"And the Mayor?"

"Forty-three."

"Who was mayor when the Germans arrived in 1940?"

"Dr. Nobel. He remained mayor for ten years after the war."

"Is he dead?"

"No. In spite of his age, he still practices in his old house on the Grand-Place."

Three minutes later Maigret had Dr. Nobel on the line, and Madame Barillard listened in amazement.

"Excuse me, Doctor. This is Superintendent Maigret from the Police Judiciaire. It's not about one of your patients, but an old story that might cast a light on some recent events. It was the station of Douai, wasn't it, which was bombed in broad daylight in 1940 while several refugee trains were there and hundreds of other refugees were waiting?"

Nobel had not forgotten what had been the event of his life.

"I was there, Superintendent. It's the most appalling recollection a man can have. All was quiet. The reception committee was giving food to the Belgian and French refugees whose trains were going south.

"The women with babies were gathered in the first-class waiting room, where bottles and clean clothes were distributed. About ten nurses were at work.

"As a rule, nobody was allowed to leave the train, but the refreshments proved too tempting. Anyhow, there were people everywhere.

"And suddenly, just as the sirens started shrieking, the station shook, the glass roof broke, people screamed, and it was impossible to realize what was going on.

"It is still not known how many bombs there were.

"The scene was as ghastly outside as in, by the station and on the platforms: mutilated bodies, arms, legs, wounded people with crazed eyes rushing around gripping their chests or their stomachs.

"I was lucky enough not to be hit and I tried to turn the waiting rooms into first-aid stations. We didn't have enough ambulances or beds in the hospitals for all the wounded.

"I performed emergency operations on the spot, in worse than precarious conditions."

"You probably don't remember a tall, thin man, a Fleming, who must have had his face cut right open, and who remained deaf and dumb?"

"Why do you ask about him?"

"Because he's the one who interests me."

"On the contrary, it so happens that I remember him very well, and that I've often thought about him.

"I was there as mayor, as president of the local Red Cross and the reception committee, and, finally, as a doctor.

"In my capacity as mayor I tried to regroup the families,

identify the most seriously wounded and the dead, which wasn't always easy.

"Between ourselves, we buried several bodies which have never been identified, and, in particular, half a dozen old men who looked as though they were from a home. We later tried vainly to find out where they came from.

"In the midst of the confusion and the crowd I clearly remember one group: an entire family, an elderly man, two women, three or four children, whom the bombs had literally torn to pieces.

"It was near this group that I saw a man whose head was nothing but a bleeding mass. I had him carried to a table and was surprised to find that he was neither blind nor wounded in any vital organ.

"I have no idea how many stitches I gave him. A little girl stood unharmed a few yards away, following my movements with no apparent emotion.

"I asked her if he was a member of her family, her father or her grandfather, and I don't know what she answered in Flemish.

"Half an hour later, as I was operating on a wounded woman, I saw the man walking away, followed by the little girl.

"It was a pretty flabbergasting sight in the confusion. I had wrapped the wounded man's head in an enormous bandage, with which he wandered around heedlessly in the middle of the crowd, and he seemed not to notice the girl who trotted along at his heels.

" 'Go and get him,' I told one of my assistants. 'He's in no condition to leave without further attention.'

"That's about all I can tell you, Superintendent. When I had time to think about him again, I inquired in vain. He had been seen wandering among the ruins and the ambulances. The stream of every sort of vehicle continued to flow in from the north, carrying furniture, families, mattresses, sometimes pigs and cows.

"One of my scouts thought he saw a tall, elderly man, slightly bent, get on a military truck together with a little girl whom the soldiers helped to climb in.

"During and after the war, when we tried to tidy the whole thing up, there were a certain number of queries. In the villages of Holland, Flanders, and the Pas-de-Calais a good many town halls had been destroyed or plundered, and the registers had been burned.

"Do you think you have found this man?"

"I'm almost sure."

"What's happened to him?"

"He's just been found hanged, and at the moment I'm sitting in front of that little girl."

"Will you let me know what happens?"

"As soon as it becomes clear. Thank you, Doctor."

Maigret mopped his brow, emptied his pipe, filled another one, and said gently to his companion:

"And now tell me your story."

She had been watching him with large anxious eyes as she bit her nails, curled up in the armchair like a little girl.

Instead of replying, she asked him bitterly:

"Why do you treat Fernand like a criminal and why have you handcuffed him?"

"We'll come to that later, if you don't mind. For the moment, it's by giving me frank answers that you are most likely to assist your husband."

Another question came to the young woman's lips, a question she seemed to have been asking herself for a long time, if not forever:

"Was Jeff mad? Jeff Claes?"

"Did he behave as though he were mad?"

"I don't know. I can't compare my childhood to any other or him to any other man."

"Start with Douai."

"Trucks, refugee camps, trains, policemen who questioned the old man—because he seemed old to me—and who, unable to get anything out of him, questioned me. Who were we? Which village did we come from? I didn't know.

"We went farther and farther, and I'm sure that one day I saw the Mediterranean. I remembered it later and I thought we'd been as far as Perpignan."

"Did Claes try to get into Spain? To get from there to the United States?"

"How could I know? He couldn't hear, couldn't speak. To understand me, he stared at my lips, and I had to repeat the same question several times."

"Why did he take you with him?"

"It was I. I've thought about it since. I suppose that seeing all my family dead around me I hung on to the nearest man, who may have looked like my grandfather."

"Why did he take your name, assuming your name really was Claes?"

"I found out later. He always kept some slips of paper in his pocket and he sometimes wrote a few words in Flemish, because he couldn't understand French yet. Nor could I. After weeks or months we ended up in Paris, and he rented a room and a kitchen in a district I have never found since.

"He wasn't poor. When he needed money he pulled out one or two gold pieces sewn in a large canvas belt under his shirt. They were his savings. We used to go a long way around to choose a jeweler's or a pawnbroker's, which he would enter furtively, afraid of being caught.

"I knew why on the day the Jews had to wear a yellow star on their clothes. He wrote his real name for me on a piece of paper, which he subsequently burned: Victor Krulak. He was a Jew from Latvia, born in Antwerp, where, like his father and his grandfather, he worked in the diamond business."

"Did you go to school?"

"Yes. The schoolchildren made fun of me."

"Did Jeff cook the meals?"

"Yes, and he was very good at grilling meat. He didn't wear a star. He was always frightened. In the police stations he was teased mercilessly because he couldn't provide the papers necessary for an identity card.

"Once, he was sent to some asylum, because they thought he was mad, but he escaped the next day."

"Was he fond of you?"

"I think he behaved like that because he didn't want to lose me. He had never been married. He didn't have any children. I'm sure he imagined God had put me in his path.

"We were twice driven back to the frontier, but he always

returned to Paris, found a furnished room with a kitchenette, either near Sacré-Coeur or in Faubourg Saint-Antoine."

"Did he work?"

"Not at this period."

"How did he spend his time?"

"He wandered around, watched people, learned to lip-read, to understand their language. One day, near the end of the war, he came home with a false identity card, which he had been trying to obtain for four years.

"He had officially become Jeff Claes, and I was his grand-daughter.

"We moved to slightly bigger rooms, not far from the Hôtel de Ville, and people came to give him work. I wouldn't be able to recognize them now.

"I went to school. I grew up and worked as a salesgirl in a jeweler's on Boulevard Beaumarchais."

"Did old Jeff get you that job?"

"Yes. He did odd jobs for various jewelers: repairs, restoration of old jewels."

"Is that how you met Barillard?"

"A year later. As a traveling salesman he should have come to see us only every three months, but he came more often, and finally waited for me at the shop door. He was handsome, very gay and lively. He loved life. It was with him, at the Quatre Sergents de La Rochelle, that I drank my first apéritif."

"Did he know you were Jeff's granddaughter?"

"I told him I was. I told him about our adventure. Since he was going to marry me, he naturally asked to meet him. We got married and we went to live in a little house in Fontenay-sous-Bois, taking Jeff with us."

"Did you ever see Palmari there?"

"Our former neighbor? I don't know, because I've never met him since we've been here. Fernand sometimes brought home a few friends, charming men who liked laughing and drinking."

"And the old man?"

"He spent most of his time in a toolshed at the foot of the garden, where Fernand had set up a workshop for him."

"You never suspected anything?"

"What should I have suspected?"

"Tell me, Madame Barillard, does your husband usually get up during the night?"

"Never really."

"He doesn't leave the apartment?"

"Why?"

"Before going to bed, do you have some kind of tea?"

"Verbena, sometimes camomile."

"Did you wake up last night?"

"No."

"Could you show me your bathroom?"

It was not large, but quite bright and gay, with yellow tiles. Over the washbasin was a medicine chest. Maigret opened it, examined a few bottles, and kept one in his hand.

"Do you take these pills?"

"I don't even know what they are. They've been there for ages. I remember! Fernand couldn't sleep and a friend recommended these pills."

But the label was new.

"What's going on, Superintendent?"

"Last night, as on many other nights, you took a certain

amount of this drug with your tea, without knowing it, and you slept heavily. Your husband went to get Jeff in his attic and went down with him to the cellar."

"To the cellar?"

"Where a workshop had been installed. He hit him with a piece of lead piping or some similar object and then hanged him from the ceiling."

She screamed but did not faint. Instead, she started running, into the living room, where she said in a shrill voice to her husband:

"It isn't true, is it, Fernand? It isn't true you did that to old Jeff?"

Curiously enough she had her former Flemish accent.

Without giving them time to become emotional, Maigret took Barillard into the study and signaled to Janvier to watch the young woman. The evening before, the two men had been in the same study, but they were now in different places. Today it was the Superintendent who sat enthroned in the revolving chair and the saleman who sat in front of him, less caustic than at the previous interview.

"It's cowardly!" he muttered.

"What's cowardly, Barillard?"

"To pick on a woman. If you had any questions to ask, you could have asked me, couldn't you?"

"I haven't any questions to ask you because I already know the answers. You suspected that, after our talk yesterday, which was why you thought it necessary to silence the man you considered the weak point in your organization.

"After Palmari, Victor Krulak, known as Jeff Claes. A poor

old man with a feeble mind who would have done anything to be near the little girl who had put her hand in his on a day of doom. You're a swine, Barillard."

"Thank you."

"You see, there are swine and swine. With some of them, like Palmari, for instance, I can shake hands. You yourself are the worst kind, the kind one can't look at without wanting to punch or to spit."

And the Superintendent really had to control himself.

"Go ahead! I'm sure my lawyer will be delighted."

"In a few minutes you'll be taken to the Central Police Station, and this afternoon probably, or this evening, or to-morrow, we'll resume our conversation."

"In front of my lawyer."

"At the moment there's someone to whom I owe a visit which might take a fairly long time. You know whom I mean. Well, it's largely on this visit that your future will depend.

"Because now that Palmari's liquidated, there are only two of you left at the top of the pyramid: Aline and you.

"I now know you were both going to leave at the first chance, after having discreetly removed Manuel's hoard.

"Aline ... Fernand ... Aline ... Fernand ... When I next see you, I'll know which of you is—I won't say guilty, because you both are—but the real instigator of the double deed. Understand?"

Maigret called:

"Janvier! Will you take the gentleman to the Central Police Station? He has the right to dress decently, but don't let him out of your sight for a second. Have you got a gun?"

"Yes, Chief."

"There must be swarms of inspectors downstairs, and you'll find a man to go with you. See you later."

On his way out he stopped in front of Madame Barillard.

"Don't blame me, Mina, for the pain you have been and will be caused."

"Did Fernand kill him?"

"I'm afraid so."

"But why?"

"You'll have to get this idea into your head sooner or later: because your husband's a blackguard, you poor little thing. And because in the apartment opposite he found his mate."

He left her in tears, and a few minutes later he entered the cellar, where searchlights had replaced the yellow bulb. It was as though they were shooting a movie.

Everyone was talking at once. The photographers were at work. The bald doctor was demanding silence, and Moers could not get to the Superintendent.

The little Magistrate found himself next to Maigret, who dragged him into the open air.

"How about a glass of beer, sir?"

"I wouldn't say no if I could get by."

They slipped by as best they could. The death of old Jeff, who was almost unknown, had not gone as undetected as that of Manuel Palmari, and in front of the building a crowd had gathered that two policemen could hardly keep back. Reporters pursued the Superintendent.

"Nothing this morning, boys. After three, at the Quai."

He took his stout companion to Chez l'Auvergnat, where some regular customers were already lunching and it was cool.

"Two beers."

"What are you going to do about this, Maigret?" asked the Magistrate, mopping his brow. "Apparently they're uncovering all the modern implements for cutting diamonds in that cellar. Were you expecting it?"

"I've been searching for this workshop for twenty years."

"Are you serious?"

"Very serious. I knew how all the other pawns in the game worked. To your health!"

He slowly emptied his glass and put it on the bar, murmuring:

"The same again."

Then, his face still set:

"I should have understood yesterday. Why didn't I remember that story about Douai? I sent my men in every direction except the right one, and when it finally occurred to me, it was too late."

He watched the owner pour him a second beer. He breathed heavily, like a man restraining himself.

"What are you going to do now?"

"I've sent Barillard to the Central Police Station."

"Have you questioned him?"

"No. It's too soon. I have someone to question before him . . . right now."

He looked out of the restaurant at the building across the street, in particular at a certain window on the fourth floor.

"Aline Bauche?"

"Yes."

"In her apartment?"

"Yes."

"Wouldn't she be more impressed in your office?"

"She isn't impressed anywhere."

"Do you think she'll confess?"

Maigret shrugged his shoulders, was about to order a third beer, decided not to, and held out his hand to the nice little Magistrate, who looked at him with both admiration and a certain anxiety.

"See you later. I'll let you know."

"I may be lunching here, and, as soon as they've finished across the street, I'll go back to the Palais de Justice."

He didn't dare add:

"Good luck!"

His shoulders hunched, Maigret crossed the street and looked once more at the window on the fourth floor. The crowd made way for him, and only one photographer had the presence of mind to take a picture of the Superintendent charging in.

CHAPTER
7

When Maigret knocked noisily at the door of what used to be Manuel Palmari's apartment, he heard irregular steps within, and it was Inspector Janin who opened the door, looking, as usual, as though he had been caught at something. Janin was a skinny fellow, and when he walked he flung out his left leg. Like certain dogs, he always seemed to expect to be beaten.

Was he afraid the Superintendent would upbraid him for not having his jacket on, a grimy shirt open on his thin and hairy chest?

Maigret hardly looked at him.

"Anyone used the telephone?"

"I did, Chief, to tell my wife . . ."

"Have you had lunch?"

"Not yet."

"Where is she?"

"In the kitchen."

Maigret charged on. The apartment was in a mess. In the kitchen Aline was smoking a cigarette in front of a plate where some fried eggs had left unappetizing traces. This woman bore no resemblance to the spruce and fresh Aline, the "little lady," who dressed carefully in the morning to do her shopping in the neighborhood.

She must have been naked under the old blue dressing gown, its silk sticking to the perspiration on her body. Her black hair had not been combed, her face not made up. She had not had a bath, and she gave off a spicy smell.

It was not the first time that Maigret had noticed this phenomenon. He had known plenty of women as coquettish and elegant as Aline who, from one day to the next, left to themselves by the death of husband or lover, had let themselves go in this way.

Their tastes, their attitudes suddenly changed. Their clothes became gaudier, their voices more vulgar; they used language they had long tried to forget, as though their natural instincts were getting the upper hand.

"Come."

She knew the Superintendent well enough to realize that this time he was in earnest. Nevertheless, she got up slowly, extinguished her cigarette in the greasy plate, put the pack in her dressing-gown pocket and went toward the refrigerator.

"Are you thirsty?" she asked after a second.

"No."

She did not insist, but grabbed a bottle of brandy and a glass out of the closet.

"Where are you taking me?"

"I told you to come, with or without the brandy."

He made her cross the living room, pushed her roughly into Palmari's little room, where the wheelchair still evoked the presence of the old gang leader.

"Sit down, lie down, or stay standing . . ." muttered the Superintendent, taking off his jacket and searching for his pipe in his pocket.

"What's happened?"

"It's all over; that's what's happened. The moment of reckoning has come. Do you understand that?"

She was sitting on the edge of the yellow sofa, her legs crossed, while her shaky hand tried to light the cigarette she held between her lips.

She didn't care if she exposed a part of her thigh. Maigret didn't care either. Whether she was dressed or naked, the time was gone when she could appeal to a man.

The Superintendent was witnessing a sort of collapse. He had known her sure of herself, frequently arrogant, teasing him in an acid tone or insulting him in such terms that Manuel had to intervene.

He had known her when she was naturally beautiful, and her slight smell of the streets had made her exciting.

He had known her in tears, as a grief-stricken woman, or as an actress feigning grief so well that he was taken in by it.

Now all that was left was a sort of hunted animal, crouching, smelling of fear and wondering what would happen to it.

Maigret fiddled with the wheelchair, turned it this way and that, finally sat down on it in the position in which he had often seen Palmari.

"He lived here three years, imprisoned by this instrument."

He was speaking as if to himself, his hands groping for the controls of the chair, which he turned to right and left.

"You were his only link with the outside world."

She turned her head away, upset by seeing a man of Manuel's build in his chair. Maigret went on, as though she were not there.

"He was a criminal of the old school, a criminal leader. And those old men were suspicious in a different way from todays young. Above all, they never let women interfere in their business, except to exploit them. Manuel had gone beyond that stage. Are you listening?"

"I'm listening," she stammered like a little girl.

"The truth is that late in life the old crocodile started to love you like a schoolboy, to love a girl he'd picked up on Rue Fontaine, by a shady hotel.

"He'd put aside a hoard with which he could have retired to the banks of the Marne or somewhere in the South.

"The poor fool thought he was going to make a real lady out of you. He dressed you up like a housewife. He taught you how to behave. He didn't have to teach you how to count, because you learned that at birth.

"How tender you were with him! Daddy this. Daddy that. How do you feel, Daddy? Don't you want me to open the window? Aren't you thirsty, Daddy? A little kiss from Aline?"

Suddenly getting up, he growled:

"Bitch!"

She did not flinch, did not budge. She knew that in his anger he could have slapped her, or even punched her.

"Did you get him to put the buildings in your name? And the bank accounts? It doesn't matter! As long as he was here, stuck between four walls, you met his accomplices, you gave them instructions, you collected the diamonds. You still have nothing to say?"

The cigarette fell from her fingers and, with the toe of her slipper, she crushed it out on the carpet.

"How long have you been the mistress of that peacock Fernand? One year, three years, a few months? The hotel on Rue de l'Etoile was very convenient for your apointments.

"And one day, somebody, one of you two, Fernand or you, got impatient. However disabled he was, Manuel was still strong, and he could have lived another ten or fifteen years.

"His hoard was big enough for him to want to end his days elsewhere, in some place where he could be wheeled around the garden, where he could feel he was in the country.

"Was it you or Fernand who couldn't stand the idea? Speak up, but be quick."

He walked heavily from one window to the other, occasionally looking into the street.

"I'm listening."

"I haven't got anything to say."

"Was it you?"

"I have nothing to do with it."

And, as if with an effort:

"What have you done with Fernand?"

"He's at the Central Police Station, where he's cooling his heels waiting for me to question him."

"Did he say anything?"

"It doesn't matter what he said. I'll put it another way. You didn't kill Manuel with your own hands, of course. Fernand did it while you were out doing your shopping. As for the second crime . . ."

"What second crime?"

"You really don't know there's been another death in the building?"

"Who?"

"Come on! Use your head, if you aren't acting. Palmari was out of the way. But Barillard, whom no one had ever suspected, was suddenly implicated by the police.

"Before being taken to the Quai des Orfèvres and faced with each other, you were both left in your traps, you here, the man opposite with his wife, with no communication with the outside, no communication between you.

"And what happened? You went from your bed to a chair, from the chair to the kitchen, where you nibbled something without even bothering to wash.

"He wondered how much we knew. And, above all, he wondered who could provide evidence and give him away. For one reason or another, he wasn't frightened that you'd talk. Only, upstairs in the attic, there was a confederate who might be slightly mad, or cleverer than he seemed, and who might squeal."

"Is old Jeff dead?" she stammered.

"You didn't have any doubts about his heading the list, did you?"

She stared at him, baffled, not knowing what to hang onto.

"What do you mean?"

"He was found hanged this morning in Barillard's cellar, which had long since been turned into a workshop where Jeff Claes, or, rather, Victor Krulak, recut stolen jewels.

"He didn't hang himself. Somebody went upstairs to get him. He was taken down to the cellar, where he was killed before having a noose slipped around his neck."

He took his time, never looking the young woman in the eyes.

"At the moment, it's no longer a matter of burglaries, precious stones, or who slept with whom in the Hôtel Bussière. It's a matter of two murders, or two killings, both committed in cold blood, with premeditation. At least one head is at stake."

Unable to stay seated any longer, she got up and started walking up and down in her turn, taking care not to go too near the Superintendent.

"What do you think?" he heard her murmur.

"That Fernand is a wild beast and you're his mate. That you've lived here for months and years with the man you called Daddy, and who trusted you, while you were waiting for the chance to get into bed with that rat.

"That you must each have been as impatient as the other. It doesn't much matter who held the gun that killed Manuel."

"It wasn't me."

145

"Sit here."

He pointed to the wheelchair, and she stiffened, her eyes opened wide.

"Sit here!"

He suddenly grabbed her arm to make her sit where he wanted her.

"Don't move. I'm going to put you exactly where Manuel spent most of the day. Here! That's it! So as to have the radio within reach of one hand and the magazines within reach of the other. Is that right?"

"Yes."

"And where was the gun without which Manuel never moved?"

"I don't know."

"You're lying, because you said Palmari put it there every morning after having taken it into his room at night. Is that true?"

"Maybe."

"It's not maybe, damn it! It's the truth! You're forgetting I came here twenty or thirty times to talk to him."

She sat rooted to the chair where Manuel had died, her face colorless.

"Now listen to me carefully. You went out to do your shopping, all spruced up, after kissing Daddy on the forehead and giving him a last smile from the living room doorway.

"Suppose that at that moment the weapon was still in its place behind the radio. Fernand came in with his key, because he had a key, which enabled him to contact the boss when it was necessary.

"Look at the furniture well. Can you imagine Fernand

146

going around the chair and sliding his hand behind the radio to seize the gun and fire a bullet into Manuel's neck?

"No, my dear. Palmari was no choirboy and he'd have had his suspicions after the first movement.

"You see, the truth is that when you kissed Daddy, when you smiled at him, when you tripped out with the step of a smart and pretty young woman, waggling your little behind, the gun was in your handbag.

"It was all timed. In the hallway you simply had to pass it to Fernand, who was coming out of his apartment as if by chance.

"While you got into the elevator and went to do your shopping—nice red meat, vegetables smelling of the kitchen garden—he stayed at home waiting for the agreed-on time.

"It wasn't necessary to go around the old man's chair and slip an arm between him and the radio.

"A quick movement after a few words. I know how carefully Manuel kept his weapons. The gun was well oiled, and I'm sure we'll find traces of that oil in your handbag."

"It isn't true!" she shouted, rushing at Maigret, beating his shoulders and face with her fists. "I didn't kill him! It was Fernand! He did everything! It was all his idea!"

Without bothering to ward off the blows, the Superintendent merely called:

"Janin! Will you take care of her?"

"Shall I handcuff her?"

"Until she calms down. Ah! Let's put her on this sofa. I'll send up some food, and I'll try to get some lunch myself. Then she'll have to dress, or we'll have to dress her."

CHAPTER
8

"A beer to start with."

The little restaurant still smelled of the luncheon cooking, but the paper tablecloths had vanished from the tables, and there was only one customer, reading a newspaper in the corner.

"Could your waiter take two or three sandwiches and a bottle of red wine across the street, to the apartment on the left of the fourth floor."

"How about you? Have you had lunch? Is it all over?

"Would you like some sandwiches, too? Cantal ham?"

Maigret felt damp under his clothes. His massive body was empty, his limbs limp, rather like someone who has just been fighting a high fever and has suddenly recovered.

For hours he had been charging ahead, unaware of the familiar scenery surrounding him, and he would hardly have been able to tell what day it was. He was surprised to see that the clock said half past two.

What had he forgotten? He vaguely realized he had missed an appointment, but which one? Oh, yes! Gélot, on Avenue des Gobelins, who must have made out the list of jewelers visited by Fernand Barillard.

All that was over. The list would come into use later, and the Superintendent thought of the little Magistrate, for weeks to come summoning witness after witness to his untidy office, gradually compiling a thicker and thicker file.

The world returned to life around Maigret. He heard the noises of the street again, found the shimmer of the sun again, and slowly relished his sandwich.

"Is the wine good?"

"A bit hard for some, but that's because it hasn't been fiddled around with. It's straight from my brother-in-law, who produces only about twenty bottles a year."

He had some of the same wine sent to Janin, and when he left Chez l'Auvergnat he no longer looked like a menacing bull.

"When will my house return to normal?" complained the concierge as he went by.

"Very soon, very soon, my dear lady."

"And do I still have to pay the rent to the young lady?"

"I doubt it. The Examining Magistrate will decide."

The elevator took him up to the fourth floor. First he rang

at the door on the right, which Madame Barillard opened, her eyes red, still wearing her flower-patterned dress of the morning.

"I've come to say good-bye, Mina. Forgive me for calling you that, but I can't help thinking of the little girl who, in the hell of Douai, put her hand into the hand of a man with a bleeding face walking away and not knowing where he was going. You didn't know where he was taking you either."

"Is it true, Superintendent, that my husband is a . . . ?"

She did not dare say the word: murderer.

He nodded.

"You're young, Mina. Have courage!"

Madame Barillard's lips quivered, and she managed to murmur:

"Why didn't I notice anything?"

She suddenly fell on Maigret's chest, and he let her weep her fill. One day, no doubt, she would find a new support, another hand to hold.

"I promise I'll come back and see you. Look after yourself. Life goes on."

Opposite, Aline was sitting on the edge of the sofa.

"We're leaving," said Maigret. "Would you like to get dressed, or would you rather come as you are?"

She looked at him like someone who has thought a great deal and has made a decision.

"Will I see him?"

"Yes."

"Today?"

"Yes."

"Can I talk to him?"

"Yes."

"As much as I like?"

"As much as you like."

"Can I have a shower?"

"Provided you leave the bathroom door open."

She shrugged her shoulders. She didn't much care who saw her. For almost an hour she devoted herself to getting ready to go, undoubtedly in the most meticulous way ever.

She took the trouble to wash her hair and dry it with an electric drier, and took some time to select a simple black satin dress.

All the while, she continued to look firm and determined.

"Janin! Go and see if there's a car downstairs from the Quai."

"Going, Chief."

For a moment Maigret and the young woman were alone in the living room. She put on her gloves. The sun flooded in through the two windows opened onto the street.

"Admit you had a soft spot for Manuel," she murmured.

"In a way, yes."

After hesitating she added, without looking at him:

"For me, too, didn't you?"

And he repeated:

"In a way."

After which he opened the door, shut it after them, and put the key in his pocket. They took the elevator down. There was an Inspector at the wheel of the black car. Janin, standing on the sidewalk, did not know what to do.

"Go home and sleep ten hours on end."

"If you think my wife and children will let me sleep! Thanks all the same, Chief."

Vacher was at the wheel, and the Superintendent whispered a few words to him. He then got into the back seat next to Aline. After about a hundred yards the young woman, who was looking out, turned to her companion:

"Where are we going?"

Instead of going straight to the Police Judiciare, they were actually going down Avenue de la Grande-Armée and around Place de l'Etoile to go down the Champs-Elysées.

She took it all in eagerly, knowing she might very well never see this sight again. And if she ever saw it again, she would be a very old woman.

"Did you come this way on purpose?"

Maigret sighed without replying. Twenty minutes later she followed him into his office, which the Superintendent reoccupied with evident pleasure.

He automatically put his pipes in order, went to the window, and finally opened the door to the inspectors' office.

"Janvier!"

"Yes, Chief."

"Will you go down to the Central Police Station and bring back Barillard? Sit down, Aline."

He now treated her as though nothing had happened. One would have thought he had nothing more to do with the business, that the whole case had just been an intermission in his existence.

"Hello! Let me speak to the Examining Magistrate, Monsieur Ancelin, please. Hello! . . . Hello! . . . Monsieur Ancelin? Maigret here . . . I'm at my office, yes. . . . I've just arrived with a young woman whom you know. . . . No, but it soon will . . . I wonder if you'd like to witness the encounter. . . . Yes . . . Right now. I'm expecting him at any moment."

He was about to take off his jacket, but he did not do it on account of the Magistrate.

"Nervous?"

"What do you think?"

"That we're going to see a fight of wild beasts."

The woman's eyes glinted.

"If you were armed I wouldn't stake much on his life."

The sprightly little Magistrate was the first to arrive, and he looked with interest at the young woman in black who had just sat down.

"Sit in my chair, sir."

"I don't want . . ."

"Please do. My part is almost over. I've only got a few things to check, some witnesses to question, some reports to make out and turn over to you. A week of paper work."

Steps were heard in the corridor, and Janvier knocked at the door and pushed Fernand, in handcuffs, into the office.

"As for these two, they're yours from now on."

"Shall I take his handcuffs off, Chief?"

"I don't think that's wise. You stay here. I'll make sure there are some strong fellows next door."

Aline had got up with a start, as though she had scented the man who had long been her lover.

Not her lover: her mate. Just as she had been his.

They were two animals looking at each other, in this peaceful office, just as they would have looked at each other in an arena or in the jungle. Their lips quivered, their nostrils contracted. Fernand began to hiss:

"What have you . . ."

Standing in front of him, her chest thrown out, her muscles taut, she thrust forward a face filled with hate and spat at him.

Without wiping the spit off, he, too, stepped forward, his hands in front of him, threateningly, while the little Magistrate fidgeted, ill at ease in Maigret's chair.

"You bitch, you . . ."

"Swine! . . . Rat! . . . Murderer! . . ."

She managed to scratch his face, but in spite of his handcuffs he seized her arm in midair and twisted it, leaning over her, his eyes full of all the hatred in the world.

Maigret, standing between his office and the inspectors', gave a sign, and two men rushed in to separate the couple, now rolling on the floor.

For a few seconds there was a scuffle, and finally Barillard, his face bleeding, was pulled up, and Aline, in handcuffs, was pushed over to a chair.

"I think it'll be all right to interrogate them separately, Monsieur Ancelin. The most difficult thing of all won't be to make them talk, but to stop them talking."

Monsieur Ancelin got up, led the Superintendent to the window, and, leaning toward him, murmured, still shaken by what he had just seen:

"I've never seen such a display of hatred, such an explosion of brutality!"

Over his shoulder Maigret said to Janvier:

"You can lock them up!"

And he added, ironically:

"Separately, of course."

He did not watch them leave, turned as he was to the peaceful face of the Seine. On the banks he looked for a familiar figure, the figure of a fisherman. He had called him "his" fisherman for years, although it was probably not always the same one. What mattered was that there was always a man fishing near the Pont Saint-Michel.

A tug pulling four barges moved upstream and lowered its funnel to pass under the stone arch.

"Tell me, Maigret, which of the two, do you think . . ."

The Superintendent lit his pipe before he said, still looking out:

"You're the magistrate, aren't you? I can only let you have them as they are."

"It wasn't a pretty sight."

"No, it wasn't a pretty sight. It wasn't a pretty sight in Douai, either."

Epalinges, March 9, 1965